What others are saying MW00883058

"The funniest book I've read in years! I actually shot milk out my nose."

-Will Ferrell's second cousin

"If I could take only one book to the moon with me, it'd be this one. Either this one or that other one, but I forgot the other one's name, so I guess I'd take this one."

-Neil Armstrong's neighbor

"...tour de force...rampage...laugh riot."

-Salmon Rushdie's laundress

"Sandoval's a real hoot. I've read all her stuff. Oh, this is the only one? Then, yes, I've read all her stuff."

-Tina Fey's third grade teacher

"You can't go wrong with it...the comedic timing is amazing; the humorous sophistication of the thing is stunning. I just love everything about Dorothy Parker. Who? Sandoval? Never heard of him."

-Vladimir Nabokov's dentist

"Brilliant! Shocking display of tremendous humor! Of great import! Must be read to be believed! I had a whale of a time!"

-le jardinier de David Sedaris

This Book Is

Funny

by

Michelle Sandoval

Table of Contents

Cave with a View

"**A**nd this is the great room. As you can see, it offers plenty of living space, what with the fire pit in the middle and the ample seating area."

John did a 360 in the middle of the room and took it all in. It was the twelfth cave he'd viewed that week, and quite frankly, he was getting tired. The agent his wife had insisted on choosing was a forceful woman who leaned toward leopard print and seemed determined to shove every dwelling they viewed down their throats, thus ridding herself of what she said were their "impossible desires, considering today's housing market" and pocketing her tidy sum, which appeared would be at least half a mastodon.

"Yes. Yes, this is a fantastic room. But the view..." He gestured through the opening, his frustration building. The last cave she suggested faced due east, and the rising sun would surely wake the baby, whose early dawn cries might alarm the nearby animals, thereby severely limiting their breakfast options. This one faced a neighboring cave, and the inhabitants appeared messy. The front yard was littered with discarded stone tools and half a rotted short-faced bear carcass. Every now and then, he caught a whiff of their cooking. Neolithic. He hated foreign food.

"There's nothing wrong with that view, Mr. Rockwell. It would do you a world of good to have neighbors. Just think of the hunting buddies. And they have kids! I assure you, they're longterm renters so there's nothing to worry about."

"Renters?"

"Oh, don't be a snob. Did you check out the interior design? The last couple did a fantastic job on the paintings, don't you think? Just look at that graceful buffalo herd. You can almost smell the barbecue."

John did like the cave paintings. They were a bit rustic for his taste, but a vast improvement on the series of hand prints where they lived now. His wife, Lydia, considered herself an aspiring artist, but she'd been stuck in what she called her "hand print period" for over five years, and he yearned for something new. Perhaps with the walls already decorated, he could break her habit. Besides, he was tired of having to explain his wife's blood red palms to everyone.

"Well... I don't know. The bathroom is a bit close to the cave opening. I mean, look at that." He waved toward the stand of brush not 50 feet from them, where a man he supposed was from the rental was squatting, his face scrunched and red. "And you know I'm not keen on a community toilet."

"Oh, that." The agent waved it off. "You must understand, Mr. Rockwell, the population is exploding. Why, just yesterday during our department meeting, my boss was telling us that they fully expect the world population to hit 8,500 people by the end of the year! Do you know how many caves we need to house all those people? And don't even get me started on private bathrooms. If you want a private bathroom, an extended fire pit, quality cave paintings, and that vaulted ceiling Lydia's dreaming about, you're talking at least an increase in price of about...." here, she reached up and scratched her lice, "a half dozen antelope."

"What?"

"Yes, that's right. Although there is something on the other side of the ridge within your range that has a private bath and vaulted ceilings. And it does have a southern exposure, but. ..."

John's unibrow shot up. "Well, why aren't you showing me that?"

She shuffled her feet and hesitated. "It's a bit of a fixer-upper, and it's been empty awhile. The last inhabitants met, shall we say, an early demise."

"Neighboring tribe?"

"Saber tooth."

John cringed and felt the hair on his back stand up. "Saber tooth!"

"Yes, but that was at least seven or eight moons ago, and there haven't been any sightings since then."

"Still, I'd have a hard time convincing Lydia. Her mother lost her left foot to a saber tooth and we've been dragging her around ever since. It's been a real inconvenience."

"As I can well imagine." She paused. "You'd like to see it, wouldn't you?"

"Would you think I was crazy?"

"No, I wouldn't. Now that I think of it, it could be just the place for your little family. There's a sandpit out back and some great vines for swinging. And the walls are done in a lovely wild horse motif. Fire pit is large but could use a few more rocks. Let me just grab my club and we'll walk over. We'll be there and back before sundown."

"Do you mind if I quick whittle a spear or something? Maybe we'll be able to squeeze in a little dinner after."

"Sounds good to me. I spotted a sloth out back a few days ago. I'm sure he's still there. "

"Great. My baby loves sloth. The toes are a special treat, as he is teething."

The agent grabbed her trendy bog lemming skin satchel bag and swung it over her shoulder. "Then let's get going. If this location works for you, perhaps we can get in an offer and have you settled in before the holidays. Lydia tells me her whole family is coming this year!"

"She did, did she? Would the cave happen to come with a tar pit?"

Are You Serious?!

HOST: I'm Arnold Spitfyre, and this is 'Are You Serious?!' The game show where you have to guess what's real and what's not! Our judges carefully scan your friends' and family's Facebook, Twitter, and other social media pages for the goods on YOU! You guess what's real and what's a bunch of bunk.

And here with us today is our next very lucky contestant, Rheinhold Skyflarken. Rheinhold, how are ya, buddy?

RHEINHOLD: I'm...I'm just fine, Arnold. Thanks.

HOST: That's great, just great. Are you ready to play?

RHEINHOLD: I think so, yes.

HOST: Fantastic. Let's get started, shall we? Now, you know the rules. We'll read three bits of gossip about you. One of them our experts have gleaned off a social media site, and the other two we pulled right out of our asses. You have to guess which one is the real deal. Ready?

RHEINHOLD: Yes, I suppose that I am.

HOST: Wonderful. Here are the first three statements about you.

Number one, from your girlfriend's Facebook timeline: 'Rheinhold borrowed my car...and got a parking ticket with it again! I think I should just dump that little shit.'

Number two, from your first grade teacher's Linked In profile: 'I loved every minute of my 40 years of teaching at Martin Luther King Jr. Elementary. All of it. Except the year I had Rheinhold Skyflarken as a student. He was really stupid.'

Wow, that's harsh! And here's Number three, from your mother's Twitter feed: 'Just got a call from my son. He asked to borrow $$ for tickets to La Boheme. I'm pretty sure he's gay. Why won't he admit it already?'

Which is it, Rheinhold? Girlfriend wants to dump you, teacher thought you were stupid, or mother thinks you're gay?"

RHEINHOLD: Oh...oh boy, those are tough. Really? My girlfriend called me a little shit? I mean, I did get a parking ticket the last time I borrowed her Prius —

HOST: That's the spirit. Think it through, Rheinhold. You have 10 seconds to make your final decision.

RHEINHOLD: Okay. Well, Ms. Madison was a tough teacher. And I never felt her confidence in me. But then again, my mother keeps asking me if I'd like an ascot for Christmas."

(BZZZZT!)

HOST: Time's up, Rheiny! What'll it be for you?

RHEINHOLD: Well, I guess I'll go with my girlfriend's Facebook page.

HOST: You're....RIGHT!

(Dingdingding!)

HOST: Twenty points for 'little shit'!

RHEINHOLD: Really, though? Florence wants to dump me over a parking ticket?

HOST: Now for the bonus round.

RHEINHOLD: That hardly seems fair. I mean, I didn't get all bent out of shape when she dropped my iPhone in the toilet.

HOST: Ready, Rheinhold? This one's for double points!

RHEINHOLD: She was on vacation in Bulgaria. It was a Turkish toilet. The phone was never the same again.

HOST: Rheinhold, you must pay attention. We're about to explore your finances, as unearthed on the Internet by our team of highly trained experts. I'm sensing bankruptcy!

RHEINHOLD: The screen was fogged after that. And the smell! I can't believe this.

HOST: I think we'd better take a commercial break, let our friend pull himself together.

RHEINHOLD: And just for the record, Mom, I'm not gay.

A Page from an Amish Girl's Diary

So, I'm totally chilling out by the chicken coop, right? And my mom hands me this dumb journal with a picture on the front of it with two little kids sitting by a stream, except the kids don't have faces. 'Cause, like, I'm Amish. And she tells me that if I don't "straighten out my attitude right now, young lady," and "think very, very hard about thine actions of late," she's gonna ground me until I get married, which is, like, three whole years away because I'm only 15, which really isn't that young if you think about it 'cause I already have responsibilities and everything, like taking care of my three brothers and six sisters, four of which are twins. And that is so totally unfair because I haven't been able to go out with my friends after I gather eggs in forever!

And since I have this journal and I have to write in it anyway, like, *right now,* because she's watching me this very second to see if I'm doing it, the old hag, I might as well tell you that she already punished me once today, unless you count this stupid journal which I would, so that's punishment number two. But the first time was when she told me no more messaging my friends so she took away my homing pigeon. The joke is on her, because she thought she took my homing pigeon, but it was really Bethany's, right? Which is totally hilarious because I'd already tied a note to its foot, so when my mom threw the pigeon out the window, it took my note with it so Bethany will be all, "Oh, look, it's my pigeon and here's a note from Hester," and my mom's back at the barn tee-heeing and stuff, saying, "Oh, look, I got rid of my daughter's only contact with the outside world, aren't I evil." But really, I just wanted to tell Bethany that Matthew Yoder is all into her and wants to be her special friend and she doesn't even know it, and that she'd better drop her hankie or something soon, because Judith so has her cap set for him, I can tell you. I saw the way she was looking at him last Saturday during the barn raising, all, "He's sooo cute and he knows how to swing that hammer, and look at how he dovetails." Which is totally cool, I get it, really I do, but Bethany would look so much cuter with Matthew, I can just see their twelve kids now, all Yoderish and stuff.

And here's another thing, my mom gets her apron in a bunch just because I like to hang with Rachel Stoltzfus after council service, and who wouldn't? I have to sit behind her for three hours during service, so by then we've passed, like, a gazillion notes and we know each other super, super well. My mom, she's all, like, "Why don't you hang out with Ruthie Hershberger, and I'm, like, "Duh, her brother's a sheep's bladder and he smells like blutwurst." Plus, he hangs out by us all the time and spies on us when we're trying to make pie, which I hate to do but Ruthie has to do *every single day* because her family runs a pie stand. And the English tourists are at her house all the time, just standing there staring and trying to take pictures of us when they think we don't notice, which is so totally rude to try and steal our souls and everything, because, like, what are you going to do with an Amish soul back in Chicago? Pluck a chicken?

Besides, I can see it written all over Ruthie's face that she's gonna go all Rumshpringa any minute now, doing her teenage wild oat sewing off in Indianapolis or some such, and I'm telling you, she won't come back. She's so grossfeilich. She keeps talking about some place called Chuck E. Cheese she heard some tourist kids talking about; that and something called "Wee" or maybe it's "Us," I don't remember; some stupid game that sounds so lame but she totally wants to do it, and everything she says just gets me all ferhoodled. And I'm so not going on Rumshpringa because it is so lame unless you're into, like, shopping and driving in cars. I can't imagine leaving my horse! I mean, I have my own pony named Muslin and she's so sweet! I couldn't leave her, not for some stinky old Buick or a dirty apartment that I'd be crammed into with three other Amish girls anyway, no thanks. I already know how that is because I have to share a loft with my little sisters and they're total slobs. So I'll stay here with Muslin, thank you very much. Although, I so wouldn't mind it if Ruthie brought me back maybe a yellow bonnet with a little bee motif on it. That and some glittery shoe buckles. But don't count on it because once she sees the big city, she'll be gone, I'm telling you. She's trouble with a capital T and no one *ever* takes her homing pigeon away.

The Bumper Sticker Emporium

A man walks into a store and looks around like it's not what he expected. The store is elegant; dark hardwood walls, subdued lighting, Boston ferns on pedestals. He studies the wares for sale and appears confused by them. They're spread out on round tables like ties. He picks one up. It's a bumper sticker. He reads aloud, "My other car is a Porsche" like it's a question. He puts it back.

There's a voice from behind him, a man's voice with a clipped English accent. "May I help you, sir?"

The man spins around, caught off guard. The salesman is standing behind a glass case, and he's wearing an elegant black suit and a tie. His hair is slicked back with pomade, and he's wearing white gloves.

"Oh!" says the shopper, "No thanks, I'm just...I'm just browsing."

"Perhaps you'd like to take a look at something in the case. A hunting sticker, perhaps?"

"Well, I...I don't really hunt."

"That's too bad, sir. We have some lovely deer head silhouettes, and we just got a batch of Browning window decals in this morning." The salesman sizes up the customer, taking in his khaki pants and his button-down shirt. "Golf?"

"Huh?"

"Do you *golf*, sir?"

"No, I... I never got into it." He feels like he has to say something else. Two no's in a row is making him feel difficult. "I did play a few times, though. The golf carts are nice."

"We don't carry golf cart stickers." The salesman glances down at the man's feet. "So sorry, sir. I didn't notice the Berkenstocks. Something with a social theme, perhaps? Apartheid? The evils of fur trapping? Or how about something with a locavore slant?"

"These are my brother's Birkenstocks. We're just visiting and I accidentally dropped my shoes in a fountain over on... They're not my shoes."

"Very good, sir." The salesman takes stock once more, his keen eye combing the man for any clues. Finding nothing, he goes with his gut.

"May I interest you in our line of honor student bumper stickers? We have a wide array of accomplishments."

"Well, I do have children..."

"Here we have the 'My child is a Wilson High Honor Student.'"

"Hmm. That one is rather nice. Catchy colors. But my kids don't attend Wilson High, and they pull C's. Also, we're from Nebraska."

"How about this one: 'My child was People Person of the Month.' No? Okay, how about 'My child is smarter than your schnauzer'?

"Uh, nice sentiment, but maybe not for us." Just then, the bell above the door rings and a frazzled looking man rushes in and interrupts.

"I need a family set — and fast."

"Hello, Mr. Treacle. I know just what you're looking for." He turns to the first man and excuses himself. Then the salesman walks further down the counter and pulls out an elaborate tray of small white bumper stickers shaped like stick figures of men, women, children, dogs and cats. "What seems to be the emergency?"

The man immediately begins to riffle through the tray, pulling out people stickers and flinging them at the salesman. "We just bought a new SUV; traded the old one in. All our bumper stickers were on it!" The salesman gasps in horror. "I know! Can you believe it? We're out there just...just naked to the world! It's like everywhere we go, we're just this anonymous family in a shiny SUV. What if they think our kids are average or something? What if..." He begins to hyperventilate. The salesman puts his hand on the man's arm, knowingly. He's now in his element. He's done this before.

"There, there, Mr. Treacle. We'll have you sorted out in a jiffy. Now, what was it, two boys and a girl?"

"Yes." The man thinks a moment. "And we have a new dog."

The salesman arranges a few family stickers onto a display behind him, one that represents an unblemished back SUV window. He puts his hand to his chin and the two men look intensely at the display.

"No, no. I divorced Louise. Got a live-in girlfriend now. Jessica has long hair. Got one with long hair?" The salesman expertly switches out the women.

"Better. Can I get that one in a window cling? Not sure she'll last." Again, the salesman makes a switch.

"Mr. Treacle, are you still a member of the NRA?"

"You bet."

The salesman brings out an NRA sticker and places it in the upper right corner.

"And the Lion's Club?"

"Elk's now."

"Elk's." He adds this one to the lower right. "And let's not forget your alma mater." With a flourish, he produces a Grant Community College sticker which he puts across the top, centered perfectly.

"Ruthie's in dance now," says the man. "And Mortimer is captain of his French team."

"French! Now, that one might take me a moment." The salesman disappears behind a wall. Doors open and close as he mumbles, "French club, French club..."

Mr. Treacle turns to the other man, noticing him for the first time.

"Gee, sorry about cutting in like this. Hope you don't mind." He offers a smile of apology.

"No problemo."

"Because I was really freaked there for a

moment, you know? I mean, what if our neighbors didn't even know it was us? Can you imagine?" He laughs. "And what would the other people down at the Sam's Club think when they parked by us and didn't even know what sort of person they were next to? I tell you, just the NRA sticker alone is enough to curtail the old road rage, know what I mean? No tailgaters with *that* puppy!"

The man is about to nod in agreement when a woman in business attire enters the store. She sets her briefcase down on the counter just as the salesman returns with the French club bumper sticker. "Voila! French club." Mr. SUV says he's done, and the salesman tosses in a free BNL sticker (they were on clearance) and a Genius on Board adornment. He rings up the purchase and sends the relieved man on his way.

"Good luck," Mr. SUV says to the first man.

"I'll be with you in a moment, Ms. Haggis," says the salesman.

"I just need a fresh MENSA," she says, "in

green this time."

The salesman looks at the first man, and he nods, "It's alright." He doesn't really want to leave, not when things are getting so interesting.

"Certainly." The salesman produces a fresh MENSA sticker, as if from thin air.

"Thank you, Higgins. Just what I necessitated. The red one was simply pulchritudinous, but perhaps a bit too magniloquent. Besides, it clashed with the Beemer's paint job."

"Any time, Ma'am."

The woman left; now it was just the first man and the salesman.

"Have you found anything you'd like for your own vehicle, sir?"

"I think...you know, this seems like it'd require a bit of thought, really, and I don't...well, I'll be in town a few more days and..."

"I understand, sir. I understand completely."

The man fidgeted with a flying pig emblem for a moment before setting it down and walking out of the store. Out on the sidewalk, he found his car parked before a meter. He went to the back and stood looking at the window, devoid of embellishments. His eyes scanned the car's back end, landing on the bumper. He bent down and squinted at a small sticker on the tail end he'd never paid much attention to before. "Al's Motor World" it said. He scraped at it. He scraped at it some more. Finding a loose edge, he pulled with his nails until one corner came loose. He slowly yanked until the whole sticker came free. Then he tossed it in the gutter, got in his car, and drove back to the hotel.

The Fundraiser

And that was Peter Ignacius and his Tuba Quartet, playing, "What's for Dinner? It's a Dumpling." Thank you for joining us here at WYBS Public Radio once again. We know it's a challenge for you to listen to us during our annual Fund Raiser Week, what with all the groveling and mock sincerity, but we ask that you just stick with us a few short moments. We should be returning to more of your favorite music after a brief but enchanting change of pace. I have with us here in the studio a very special guest, 86-year-old Ms. Lilah Bloombury from the one of the station's most popular radio talk shows, "Blooming with Bloombury," which you can hear live every Saturday morning at 4:30 a.m., right after "Bob's Bassoon Cafe." Lilah is a lifelong gardener with 5 children, 12 grandchildren, and 6 great grandchildren! But she doesn't let all that busy family time get in the way of her job. Her gardening call-in show has gone from 28 listeners back in 1987 to a whopping 45 just last week. Welcome, Lilah!

THANK YOU, BETTY! IT'S SO GREAT TO BE HERE!

Oh. Wow. You are energetic, aren't you?

I'VE BEEN TOLD I'M PEPPY.

I'd say "peppy" is an apt description.

YOU HAVE TO BE PEPPY AT 4:30 IN THE MORNING, DEARY, ESPECIALLY IF YOU'RE TALKING GARDENING. BY THE WAY, THIS COMING SATURDAY WE'RE TALKING ABOUT NEMATODES.

Yes, I hear those can cause trouble if you...

BENEFICIAL NEMATODES, MY DEAR. WE'LL ALSO BE TALKING ABOUT ADDING EDIBLE BLOOMS TO YOUR SUMMER SALADS...WHAT A TREAT. AS A MATTER OF

FACT, I'M SERVING THAT ONE TO THE CHURCH CHOIR THIS WEEKEND.

Okay, then. Well, Lilah, I wanted to talk to our listeners about donating to our station this season, and I thought what better way than bringing in our very own Ms. Bloombury. Your show is such a big hit with the early weekend riser crowd and...

THAT SLOT SUCKS.

Uh...I'm so sorry to hear that, but your listeners are very grateful to you, I'm sure. As I was saying, giving to your local public station...

IF I HAVE TO DO ONE MORE SATURDAY SHOW AT THAT UNGODLY HOUR, I'LL PUT A BULLET THROUGH THE CONTROL PANEL.

Oh, haha. Ms. Bloombury, you are a feisty one. Always that sense of humor. Maybe you could tell us more about your own garden.

I DON'T HAVE TIME TO GARDEN. I HAVE ALL THOSE GRANDKIDS AND GREAT

GRANDKIDS, AND THEN THAT STUPID SATURDAY SHOW THAT I ONLY KEEP BECAUSE MY SOCIAL SECURITY CHECK IS SO PATHETIC. I COULD JUST JUMP OFF A BRIDGE.

Please don't do that. I'm sure we'd all miss you and...

RIGHT NOW. DO YOU KNOW WHERE I CAN FIND A BRIDGE?

Oh, my. Let's take a quick station break and — I can't? The station manager is making faces in the glass... oh, that's right. We don't have commercials.

I'D LIKE TO WRING HIS NECK IS WHAT I'D LIKE TO DO, DAMNED STATION MANAGER. YOU KNOW HE MADE A PASS AT ME? AN 86-YEAR-OLD WOMAN.

I'm sure he didn't mean to. SAID MY ANKLES GOT HIM WORKED INTO A LATHER. AND HE'S SO MUCH YOUNGER, WHAT ARE YOU, 73? I'M NO COUGAR, YOU BIG JERK.

Alrighty. Let's talk donations, shall we? You all know that we count on you, our listeners, to support our station. Without you...

WITHOUT YOU, I'D BE HAPPILY IN RETIREMENT, SITTING BY A POOL IN PHOENIX DRINKING A MAI TAI. WITHOUT THE GRANDKIDS.

Well. I'm sure they're lovely children, and it's children like that who deserve a good local radio sta—

LOVELY, MY ASS. THERE IS ABSOLUTELY NO DISCIPLINE IN THOSE KIDS. THE YOUNGEST GRANDDAUGHTER HAS GREEN HAIR AND A NIPPLE PIERCING.

Uh — which is exactly why our children need public radio. Donate just $50 and receive a WYBS coffee mug filled with...

BULLSHIT.

(Bob, where's the mute button? Why didn't you hit the mute button?)

THAT'S RIGHT, IT'S BULLSHIT.

(We don't HAVE a mute button? How can this possibly be?) Yes, by donating $100, we'll install a mute button or one of those bleepy things...

DAMNED GRANDKIDS. GREEN HAIR, FOR FU—

Bleeeep! Bleep-bleeeeep! WHAT ARE YOU SHOUTING FOR? WHAT, YOU THINK EVERY OLD PERSON IS DEAF? I'M RIGHT HERE.

WHAT'D YOU SAY?

I said I think it's time for our music segment now, a special rendition of "Yessir, That's my Baby" by Shirley McFee and her Magical Harpsichord.

YOU SAID THIS INTERVIEW WOULD GO FOR AN HOUR. I GOT MY HAIR DONE. I WOKE UP WHEN I SHOULD BE IN A GERITOL INDUCED COMA ON THE COUCH WATCHING MATLOCK RERUNS. WHAT A CROCK.

Well, time flies when you're having fun. Doesn't it, Bob? Let's get rockin' with that harpsichord, shall we?

GIMME THAT MICROPHONE.

No.

I'LL SHOVE A TULIP SO FAR UP YOUR NOSE YOU'LL BE DREAMING IN TECHNICOLOR.

Remember, folks, call in now and make your pledge of support to keep programming such as this...well, not exactly like this, but maybe more like Harry's Harmonica Hour, going strong! HARMONICA, MY ASS. I'LL GIVE YOU A HARMONICA.

We Were Beautiful Once

I was only 19 when I landed the part of Ursula in the musical version of *Sailors on Holiday!* The year was 1948, and I had a set of gams that in today's market would be insured for large sums, I'm certain. Was I a pinup girl? I should have been, darling. I should have been. But I had a lousy agent and he thought pinups would make me seem cheap. Why he didn't think kicking up my heels on a staged war ship surrounded by drunken sailors was cheap, I'll never know. Perhaps he was just lazy. But that's neither here nor there.

Sailors on Holiday! was my first film, but it wasn't my last. Which is fortunate. Because that one opened on V-Day, something we couldn't have predicted, and so on opening day it was already outdated. No one wanted to see Adolph Hitler anymore, even if he was bursting out into song and doing quite an impressive bit of soft shoe in front of a Howitzer. Too bad, too, because I was starring opposite Johnny Milfield in his first and last film. Such a handsome fellow. We had a fling during the filming, did you know? Last I saw of him, he was balding and covered in more age spots than an overripe banana.

My next film turned out to be a bit more timely. It was called *Mistress of the Alien Zoo*, 1953. Yes, I'm sure you've noticed the time gap there. Again, chalk that up to a lazy agent. But I looked stunning wrapped in tinfoil, and one reviewer of a not-so-minor film rag claimed that I "brought new meaning to the word 'alien.'" I suppose it was the spiked heels and the bright red hair that caused that sensation. At least it sure got the attention of the leading man, Bill Billingsley. Bill was a real heart throb; you should see him now, though. What a beer belly! And cataracts. I still get asked about that film all the time. Just last week, Hal, the 86-year-old fairy/makeup artist in 3B asked me if he could get another copy of my picture. Something about wanting it for drag costume inspiration. I'm not sure.

After that, there was another lag in my career which mercifully ended with the release of the 1958 film, "Daisy Gets a Doctor," in which I played a stunning collegiate hunting for her man so she can quit school, don an apron, and squirt out a multitude of children. Not my proudest moment, but the short skirts were real attention getters. It would have started quite a fashion trend, I'm sure, had the movie lasted in the theaters for more than a week. But, hey, that's the biz.

You thought I looked familiar right away, didn't you? I recognized that look in your eyes when you first walked in here. That's okay. I get that all the time, and I'm used to it. I know a lot of us starlets in our golden years have gone under the knife so many times that our eyelids flip inside out when we blink, but I haven't taken things that far. So don't feel bad that you couldn't place me right away. I could have maintained better over the years, I suppose, but cheek implants? Really? I don't want to be confused with Joan Rivers. (Lovely gal, that Joan.) At least when people stare at my cleavage and say, "Are those real?" I can shout, "Yes! The girls are real! Look but don't touch. They're taped up."

Perhaps you're also wondering about my humble accommodations. Many retired stars still live in glitzy manors, I know, but I haven't gone that route as you can see. I've chosen instead this wonderful location, Sunset Estates. It's conveniently located next door to a Walgreen's, so I can get my prescriptions filled whenever I need them. Like my Vicoden. And the Percocet. Also, we have a nice concierge here. Did you see Gregory down at the front desk? He does me small favors from time to time. Like yesterday, for instance. I'd just returned from a trip to

Walgreen's to pick up some suppositories... I mean some supper, and he opened the door for me. Because I had my hands full, you see. Put his book down to do it and everything. Then he said, "Good evening Madame." He always calls me Madame. He's never mentioned my fame, which is highly professional of Gregory. He's been properly trained in how to handle this sort of thing.

Of course, if I want to have my hair and makeup done right, all I have to do is call down to Hal in 3B, and he'll come right up here and do it for me. We talk on and on about the old days. He was in the biz too, and he's still got it. You've never seen such a collection of crimson lipsticks, and he looks stunning in them. And the face powders! Oh, my. I feel like a million bucks when he's done with me. Drape that feather boa around my shoulders, and I'm ready to dine out. There's an early bird special at Crabby's Seafood, and they give me the royal treatment there. Senior special all the time, bottomless cups of coffee, and all the extra napkins I want. I suppose that's part of being famous, and I've learned to live with it.

The hardest part is keeping the men at bay. I still wear the short skirts because that's just the sort of lady I am. I enjoy flaunting my best features. But the spiked heels have been retired for awhile now. I'm in need of something a bit more orthopedic. You can't believe how hard it is to get a fashionable pair of orthopedic shoes these days, but that's okay. Hal has a Bedazzler and we spend a lot of time attaching sequins and sparkly beads whenever I have a new pair to break in. Anyway, the key to walking seductively in orthopedics is all in the hips. Of course, you don't want to overdo it and throw anything out, but you've got to give your fans something to talk about. You never know when the paparazzi will come after you and catch you unawares, while you're stomping ungracefully down the sidewalk. Those paparazzi are tricky fellows, I'll tell you. They hide in the bushes and behind trees, and they're oh so very good at it because I've never seen them watching me, not once. Except for that one who dressed up in disguise as a Greek tourist who kept yelling something and laughing. The Greeks were always fond of my work. I would have suspected he was just remembering the comedic high jinx that took place in *Sailors on Holiday!* But then I remembered that those paparazzi are tricky and enjoy a good disguise every now and then. I was probably on the cover of some tabloid after that, but I never bother to look. It would just make me angry to read out and out lies about my sexual escapades. Really! At my age, a lady has to protect herself against that sort of thing.

Well, I'm really glad you stopped by to see me, and I'm sorry I won't be ordering any magazines from you. Also, I apologize for the mess in the living room. I was just reorganizing some of that old movie paraphernalia when you arrived. I never take it out anymore. It's amazing that you showed up when you did. I'll have to get that all shoved back into the boxes so I can get myself ready for dinner. Hal will be swinging by to help me prepare for the walk to Crabby's; he's coming with me this evening, hopefully without the leopard print smoking jacket. A lady of my standing can't be seen dining alone too often, or people will talk.

Procrastination

Here is where I planned on teaching you how to stop procrastinating, but I don't feel like it right now.

Sir Easter the Bunny

It is but a fortnight till that most magical of days. Alas, Easter is upon us! The time of the plastic egg, brightly colored sugary concoctions, the cellophane grass the cat chews on that makes for pleasantly colored hairballs. It will be my day, for I am Sir Easter the Bunny, and I have fluffed my tail and combed my whiskers to a luxurious shine in anticipation of visiting the local mall.

'Tis my vocation, hopping my way down the waxed marble floor that is my bunny trail. Past the Orange Julius stand, across from Pottery Barn where my likeness graces every window in distressed wooden tchotchke bliss. The fine establishment that is Birch Acres Mall has created for me a little bit of springtime heaven, near the anchor stores but far from the noise and chaos that is the children's romp and stomp. There each morn, I find an elegant brocaded

Easter throne, the whiffs of yesterday's kiddie vomit covered over by a hefty lacquer of Lysol. The landscapers have done a magnificent job of adding a royal flavor to my seasonal abode. I arrange my nethers and settle down, awaiting my first young visitor of the day, a wee lass of but five.

Ah, what a sight to behold! All frills and pink lace, the youngster exudes charm and youth, her Walmart bonnet at a rakish tilt above her imp-like face. The photographer opens the artificial white picket fence that surrounds us and guides her to me. The child stares at me for a moment of contemplation, no doubt admiring the delicate hue of my ears and the brilliance of my beady eyes. And then, inhaling deeply enough to circulate the air about my head, she shrieks with the terror that can only be had by five-year-old girls when stood before a six-foot rabbit in suspenders.

Her mother, standing on the other side of

the picket fence (because that is where we feel the parent belongs), cries out to her in reassuring yelps that bounce off the walls and can be heard clear as a bell over the thrumming of the Abercrombie & Fitch soundtrack. When promises of special goodies from the food court do not suffice, the small girl pulls back her cleverly shod foot and kicks me in my shin.

Here I must point out that on the off season I am an operatic tenor and am no stranger to letting go with a mighty "Aaaaahhh," so I do so at this moment and at full strength. But much to my chagrin, the tiny tike takes her own aria to a higher pitch, belting forth with an "Eeeeeee!" that has the Hallmark store cashiers rushing from their post, greeting cards and receipts still clutched in their manicured fingers, thus setting off the store's alarm. As the mall cops quickly hobble to my rescue, assuming the worst while shouting into their walkie talkies(which I find unnecessary as they are a mere three feet from one another), the entire scene which has unfolded before my eyes takes on a slow motion effect as I notice the girl grabbing hold of the photographer's tripod with a mighty grasp and with superhuman, superbaby strength, hoists it into the air. As the photographer's face contorts into an expression that can only be translated as "Oh my God, that lens set me back two grand," the entire apparatus is launched from the girl's sticky mitts and slowly, oh so slowly floats through the air toward my delicate pink rabbitty nose. I try to thwart the gear with uplifted paw but am unable to do so, so weighted do my limbs feel. Instead, there is a loud thump and all goes black. I awaken from my slumber how much later I am unable to determine. But from what I can tell by the damp and ruddy complexions of the mall cops, and the insistent wheezing sounds emanating from deep within their respiratory systems, I have been carried away from my indoor garden of Eden and taken to a faraway location, perhaps the employee break room. I am stretched across the lunch table, bits of Gatorade and Dorito cheesy goodness clinging to my now sullied fur. While the men with badges don't seem to take particular interest in my plight, the woman I recognize as the tea sample girl is caressing my aching brow and asking if I would like a Yazzoberry sample. "It will revive you," she says, but I am in no mood for tea, no, not I.

It has been, dear reader, many countless years that I have been making the long trek to the mall each Easter season. Many gay and happy photos do I appear within, smiling children on my knee, confusing me with Santa and requesting bikes and things called Squinkies, me all the while gently explaining that I bring eggs and candy only, an occasional book perhaps. For more seasons than I can count, I have brought joy and happiness to a generally large percentage of the visiting children; I can see the glow on their faces when they leave with their parting gift, a plastic chick-shaped whistle I bestow upon them, a tiny token with which to irritate their mothers for the rest of the afternoon and several days hence until said whistles magically disappear or are accidentally vacuumed up. Alas, the time has come to call it quits, to end the gig, to pack it all up and leave this, the most illustrious of jobs, the shopping mall Easter Bunny. I shall instead turn in my over sized bow tie and head south where I've dreamed of being for so long, down Mexico way where a small beach house awaits me. Yes, and there in the beach house I will spend my days and nights in enchanting tropical splendor, admiring the waves, sticking my large and paddle-like feet into the warmth of the sand, sipping fruity beverages, but not alone shall I be. For there in the beach house awaits my one true love, the only one who has ever understood this life which I have lead, my darling Lady Tooth of Fairy.

Word Pairs Rarely, If Ever, Uttered Before

My fascination with words started as soon as I could read. I have a strong memory of riding my bike and thinking in words, punctuating as I went along. I envisioned my thoughts in full sentences, starting with capital letters, having commas and periods as required. One particular thing I loved to do was to try and come up with word combinations or sentences that I was sure I was the first person in the history of the world to utter. A friend of mine and I used to make a game of it together. We'd find two seemingly unrelated words, then try and knock down the theory that they'd never, ever been used together. To do this, we'd construct sentences using the combination. If the sentence came out logically, our thought was that the sentence had probably already been used by someone at some time or another already. But if the sentence was totally nonsensical or made us choke on a pretzel, then, bingo! We'd probably just achieved a verbal groundbreaking moment.

What follows are my attempts to recapture my youth. If these combinations have ever been used together before, I'll be a buttoned wombat.

whiffle cheese

I could tell it was whiffle cheese right away, on account of all the little holes; that, and it is exceptionally light and airy.

buttoned wombat

Here at the zoo, we have a wide variety of nocturnal creatures, including the very quiet buttoned wombat.

zither stripes

I must be doing something wrong here, because whenever I practice the zither, I get zither stripes across my forearm.

mink ficus

I used to have just a regular old green ficus in the corner, but I wanted something more furry so I bought that mink ficus.

carpet face

She fell down hard and got back up with a terrible case of carpet face.

squirrel pocket

Whenever he felt like picking up trinkets on his walks, he wore his special shirt with the squirrel pocket in front.

Edsel motif

John collected old cars of all sorts, so when his wife offered to redecorate the kitchen in an Edsel motif, he was endlessly pleased.

twee redwood

After a wonderful vacation to the redwood forest, Jacqueline went straight home and knitted herself her very own twee redwood.

Butterball piccolo

He always found it especially challenging to create musical instruments out of broasted turkey, so he was extra proud of the Butterball piccolo.

pistachio palace

Some people made gingerbread houses, but Alice was different; come Christmastime, she preferred a nice pistachio palace.

eternal potato

The toddler stared down at his dinner plate, wishing he could get down and play instead of being forced to eat that doggone eternal potato.

fusion wumpus

Bill's scientific experiments were always most noisy whenever he started up all that fusion wumpus.

holistic farts

My nutritionist insists that I no longer have gas but holistic farts.

aerosol fistula

The doctor took one look at her navel spraying all over the place like that and pronounced it a severe case of aerosol fistula.

Chernobyl corpuscle

The blood vessels were strangely mutated, most of them containing things like tiny eyes, which led the lab tech to believe he was staring at the first ever Chernobyl corpuscle.

acrobatic nostril

"You know you drive me mad," she said, rushing to him in passion, her one acrobatic nostril proving she was sincere.

guppie fisticuffs

He used to keep his fish all together until the time he lost six of his favorites during a bad outbreak of guppie fisticuffs.

elite boonswaggle

The king and queen hosted raucous parties every spring, famous for a large amount of elite boonswaggle.

aromatic hornblower

Jeff loved playing the trumpet, especially after downing a glass of air freshener, thus giving him the nickname "Aromatic Hornblower."

discount cumulus

The weatherman assured everyone the

clouds were so cheaply made this morning that they were no doubt a bunch of discount cumulus.

hightower muffin

She always made her best baked goods while baking on the 98th floor, which accounted for all the dozens of hightower muffins whenever she visited Donald Trump.

beatnik truffle

Some mushrooms are especially jazzy, such as this here beatnik truffle.

The Solicitor

*A*man in a suit whistles his way up a suburban driveway to a little house and rings the doorbell. *He's carrying a leather satchel and he's brimming with confidence. The woman who opens the door (after his second insistent ring) is not amused. She's messy and looks tired, perhaps annoyed at having been interrupted.*

MAN: Hello, Ma'am. I'm sorry to disturb you...

WOMAN: Are you?

MAN: Yes, indeed. In fact, that's what I'm here for.

WOMAN: (*grimaces*) You're here to apologize for disturbing me?

MAN: (*forced laugh*) No, Ma'am, I'm here on behalf of all the solicitors you'd normally be receiving throughout the summer season. You see, I'm with a new service called (*flourishes a business card her way*) Solicitor's Friend. Instead of receiving countless interruptions from your friendly neighborhood solicitors, I will instead present each business to you, right here, right now, one at a time; therefore, getting everything over within one helpful swoop. After this, you'll have a full summer of a silent doorbell. Neighborhood children not withstanding, of course.

WOMAN: (*skeptical, eyeballing card*) I see. So you're gonna get it all over with right now, huh?

MAN: Right now.

WOMAN: Like rippin' off a Band-Aid.

MAN: If you wish.

WOMAN: Alright, give it your best shot. But I'm warning ya, I'm a tough sell.

MAN: Wonderful. Here we go.

MAN reaches into his briefcase and produces an AT&T badge.

MAN: Madame, have you heard that our new fiber optics cables have recently been installed in your area and...

WOMAN: Next! You guys come here every couple o' weeks with the update. Don't even get me started on the junk mail. Enough to kill a small rainforest.

MAN: Very good. Let's move on, shall we?

Not too difficult, is it?

WOMAN: Keep it goin'.

MAN: *(removes badge, grabs brochure)* Where are you spiritually?

WOMAN: Not going there.

MAN: (d*rops badge, picks up flower*) Hari hari?

WOMAN: Nuh-uh.

MAN: (e*xchanges flower for bible*) Every Sunday, Our Lady of Continuous Agony will be having services in a tent at Shadyside Park...

WOMAN: Look, I'm a very strict nondenominational Jewish Protestant, alright? Get a move-on.

WOMAN: Did you see this dump? I think it's pretty obvious we're not spending a dime on it, huh?

MAN: I'm working my way through college by selling these coloring books which depict actual homeless people in the area. For instance, here's a picture of Buster who lives under an I 96 bridge downtown. Each book comes with a free box of eight waxy crayons in various shades of misery so your child can experience what it might be like to panhandle each day and never bathe.

WOMAN: That's just gross.

MAN: I think we're getting somewhere, though. You really let me express myself that time!

WOMAN: Mere morbid curiosity.

MAN: (*crestfallen*) Oh. Well, how about a cookbook to help send me to Europe next summer?

WOMAN shakes her head no.

MAN: Magazine subscription so I can go to band camp?

MAN: (*sighs and puts on hardhat*) We just finished reroofing the Carbunkle's house at 455 Elm, and...

WOMAN shakes her head no.

MAN: Popcorn tin to support my little league team?

WOMAN shakes her head no.

MAN: (*reaches in bag and produces a*

dilapidated photo of a house) I'm twelve years old and live in a low income area of your neighborhood. I paint houses so I can join an after-school program where I'll learn the fine art of small business entrepreneurship.

WOMAN: Lower income than this area? Please. I can't even afford to paint my toenails.

Fade out. Fade back in. WOMAN is sitting on a folding chair in the doorway, sipping a beer, foot resting on her knee.

MAN: Girl Scout cookies? Candy bars? How's your Internet provider treating you?

WOMAN: (*stands up as if she's been sitting a long time*) Look, are you about done? Cause Jeopardy comes on at 7:00 and then it's Overeater's Island Sacrifice at 8:00.

MAN: (*looks defeated*) That's all I got. Are

you sure you won't take anything?

WOMAN: Nah, but you worked hard at it.

MAN mops his brow.

WOMAN: So I tell ya what I'm gonna do for ya. I got here (*reaches around corner*) one case of the finest PBR in town, fresh off the Sav-A-Heap shelf just this mornin'. I'm willing to give you a deal on a can for five bucks. Or you can get three for $10, but today only.

MAN looks tempted.

WOMAN: If you act now, I'll throw in a bag of pork rinds for only a buck more. Whaddya say?

(MAN *grudgingly pulls out wallet and hands woman the money. WOMAN checks the amount, puts it in her pocket, and hands over the goods. Then she slams the door. MAN sits on the front steps with an open beer and the pork rinds.)*

MAN: I'd get me a new line of work, but I come across the best deals this way.

The Fashion Critic

As your local fashion critic, I have a confession to make: I'm not getting the feeling that I'm making much of a difference here. You've got to work with me on this. I can't keep kicking out this darned weekly column if you all continue to insist upon looking the way you do. Get a full-length mirror, why don't you? And take some notes. Are yo listening? Good.

Let's set the record straight: If it's warm enough to wear shorts so tiny your butt cheeks hang out the bottom, you do not need a decorative scarf. Nor do you need large boots with heavy wool lining. It looks ridiculous and it annoys me, so you should probably not do it. Sure, if you like wearing large sunglasses that hide the majority of your face so we assume you must be too beautiful to bestow your heavenly countenance upon us, fine. Just don't pair that look with flannel pajama pants that drag in the mud. Even if you're wearing Crocs. That does not balance things out.

Bra straps? They're for under your clothes, darling. As are camisoles. What are you going to do next, put your underwear on top of your jeans? Wear your boyfriend's boxers as a sort of hat? Now, that I'd like to see. Do something original and you might find yourself going down in the annals of fashion. Doubling up on tank tops will not do this for you.

Perhaps these are regional oddities. In other parts of the country, boots with shorts would just never happen unless you're a homeless prostitute in January. But as your friendly Daily News fashion critic, I feel it's my duty to inform you of all your fashion faux pas, so as to save your being humiliated, should you, say, run into someone such as Tyra Banks. Or Justin Timberlake. Or, let me help you relate better, Justin Bieber.

And speaking of Bieber, Bieberwear is out,

out, out. In fact, it has never actually been in, so if you could just do yourself a favor and take your dirty Bieber backpack when she's sleeping, take it to the back yard and douse it with gasoline, then set it alight, you'll be correcting a great and egregious fashion flop.

Let's talk jewelry, shall we? Feathers are for birds.

Next: What's hot in footwear this season? Not your $2 flip flops.

It's top time! What's flirty and cute and goes with just about any pair of pants you own? None of my shirts, I can tell you that. Your pants collection is atrocious. Have you really looked in your closet lately? Those jeans you were so proud of three years ago when they were new and fresh from Walmart make your butt look like and exploding cupcake. And that fringy grungy stuff on the bottom that you claim you'd like to trim off one of these days, let me give you a little hint: Those pants need more than a trim. They need a shredding, dear heart. Just pull 'em off right now and hand them over.

Seriously, hand them to me now.

That's what I thought. I really didn't want to discuss your underwear today, but I can see it's not to be avoided. Where'd you get those things, GrannyButts.com? I know what you're thinking. You're thinking I'm going to make you hand those over too, but I don't have the stomach for it. Hey, if you want your ass to look like two angry dogs fighting in a wet paper sack, who am I to interfere?

Just put the pants back on. It's not like I'm going to let you borrow some of mine. Besides, there's not a pair of pants in my closet that will (a) fit you or (b) match those hideous socks. Socks with flip flops. Ugh. What are you, Japanese? (And just for the record, they have special socks for that look. Stylish ones. With cranes and fans and cherry blossoms.)

You know what? I knew the day I took this

job I was in trouble. The moment I set my Jimmy Choo clad foot into this city, I took one look around at you people, and I thought, "This is hopeless. There is no fashion here. Only faux leather NASCAR jackets and tattered sweatpants. Why'd they hire me, anyway? Who in the world pays attention to fashion here? Certainly not you. You've been reading my column for five and a half years, and the best question you've been able to throw my way has been, "Should I wear my plastic tiara with my teal cocktail dress or just keep it for casual Fridays?" Honestly, if I thought you had the slightest chance at looking glamorous, even for five minutes of your life, I'd give it all up for you. I'd finally sell my condo in Malibu, and I'd happily devote my life to making sure you know how to avoid tan lines. I'd help you choose the perfect pair of gold hoops to set off your Louis Vuitton sunglasses, which I'd make sure you knew to wear in the evenings so as to avoid getting flashbulb eye from all the paparazzi following you about.

Instead, I am packing up my Gucci bags and heading back to Malibu where I belong, where I can finally get myself a decent manicure and receive a proper colon cleanse. Because I'm feeling so backed up right now that even a new pair of Manolo Blahniks can't make me smile.

We Buy Gold

Alright, everybody, let's settle down. I realize it's an exciting time for you all, what with the new job and the prospects of your first paycheck looming in the near future, but we've got some serious training to do. So let's take our seats, shall we?

Welcome to "We Buy Gold" Store #142. I'm Bob Grapplicky, and I'm the store manager here at the West 52nd Strip Mall location. If you've got questions, I'm your man. If you've got complaints, well, there's a suggestion box in reception. But I'm warning you I don't take kindly to complainers. Or whiners. Or sissypants crybaby waa-waas. I need tough men and women out there to get the job done. Understand? Good. Glad we're on the same page.

Let's get started, shall we? I'll now introduce you to the tools of the trade. Here we have a standard issue signboard, stating that, in fact, We Buy Gold. That's right, we buy gold. This is key, people. If you don't have your sign, you don't have your job.

You might think that this job is simple, that standing outside the store for eight hours a day waving around a big yellow sign is gravy. Well, you're wrong! This is serious business, and I mean to drill that into you this afternoon. So remember these few steps: Red Bull, Spit 'n Polish, iPods.

Write that down, I'll wait.

First order of business when you arrive each day: Stop by reception and pick up your complimentary Red Bull beverage. We will not serve coffee. We will not, for the love of God, serve tea. And we will never provide water. You want those items, feel free to bring them along. But here at We Buy Gold, Red Bull is freely provided. So begin each morning by downing your Red Bull, maybe two. If you have a heart condition, remember, you signed a waiver. Best be leaving right now, this is not the job for you.

Alright, goodbye, sir. I saw you walk in here, the first thing I thought to myself is, "Anyone as pallid as that is only an inch from a massive coronary." Call it a hunch. You're welcome.

Next: Spit 'n Polish. You are responsible for your signage. That means every day after your beverage, you will be making sure your We Buy Gold sign is in pristine condition. We don't make 'em knock-your-eyes-out yellow for nothing. If it's dirty, it won't stop traffic. So shine that sign! Cleaning materials will be provided. This means any chili dogs lobbed at you the day before, any cliche rotten tomatoes, dirty disposable diapers, or (as Ted could testify to last week), Rocky Road frozen yogurt product shall be fully removed from your signage before you don your authentic '49er gold digger costume. Is that understood? Perfect!

Finally, be sure to bring along your iPod or

what have you. I highly recommend you get acquainted with some Metallica or Black Sabbath or whatever you young people listen to these days. Just make sure it is LOUD! Am I understood? Head banging while holding your sign is highly encouraged. Sleeping behind it is not. This sign, people, is not a hiding place for the sluggard. You will be in front of it in full view of the public. Anyone caught sleeping off last night's party will be shot on sight.

Of course I'm kidding.

Let's talk a little bit about your attitude, shall we? I want chipper. I want perky. I want slammin' butt-kickin' steamin' funk out there, people. Our best guy, Ted, is here to show you how it's done. Ted? You can come in now.

Notice his costume. While the sign is to be pristine at all times, the costume isn't necessarily that important. Feel free to let the pants bottoms drag in the dirt. Notice Ted's. They are shredded beyond all recognition, and this is a good thing.

What do you feel when you look at Ted's pants? You in the back.

Yes, disgust. But what we're really going for here is pity, people. Pity. You will be rocking hard out there, and some days it will be upon ice-encased pavement. Other days it will be beneath the blistering waves of the midsummer sun. We want people to take pity on you. This helps them feel connected with you on a much deeper level than just as a fellow rocker. They will feel so sorry for you that they will bring in their grandfather's gold pocket watch and sell it to us at an astounding loss just to erase the image of you and your filthy pants from their tortured minds.

Next. Let's take a look at Ted's official We Buy Gold 49ers hat. Now, as you know, 1849 was the gold rush. No? I see a look of confusion cast about the room. Let's just take my word for it, shall we? Gold rush. 1849. This is an oversized caricature of the hats popularized by the rough and ready men who forged a trail to Cal-i-for-nieay to make their fortune in gold. Notice that Ted's does not fit properly. Also notice that he is wearing the hood from his hoodie sweatshirt beneath the hat. This, again, is key in cranking up the pity factor. Always let the motorists sense your discomfort. But only through the use of dirt, grime, and too many layers. Otherwise, it's perky, perky, perky.

Now, Ted, give us the dance.

Great job. Notice how Ted's earbuds are affixed to his ears. I'm sure that from where you're sitting, you can hear a tinny rendition of Feel the Love, but passersby will have the profound experience of seeing Ted here dancing to the beat of a silent drummer. It adds that wow factor we're looking for. Also notice how his head jams up and down as if on a piston of some sort. I don't recommend you go for this your first day out. Ted is an experienced 49er and can go like this for hours. But you try this without the proper training and we'll have insurance breathing down our backs over the ever increasing costs of MRIs and neck braces.

Okay, Ted. You can stop.

I don't think Ted can hear us. Janice, give him a good shake. THANKS, TED! YOU CAN GO NOW!

Let's give him a round of applause!

I think we've had enough preparation. I'm very proud of you all; this is a serious undertaking, and I can tell by the treads on your sneakers that you're ready to give it all you've got. Please don't forget to stop by reception on your way out to pick up your costumes and signage. We'll reconvene this same time next week to hear a special guest speaker, Johnny Fipper, give his rousing talk on sign swinging, high kicks, and making apathetic eye contact with angry drivers.

Happy Camper

It's spring! For many adventurous Americans, that means RV time is rolling around once more. Yes, time to pack the family up into your spacious home on wheels and hit the open road. You and your wife spent a lot of time and hard earned dollars getting that gorgeous 1997 RV prepped and repaired, and you've been planning the fun and educational trip to the Grand Canyon all winter long. Just imagine the looks on your children's small and endearing faces when they see the great expanse and the knee knocking depths of that National Wonder. Yes, it's true, you live way over on the East Coast; and yes it's true your self-absorbed boss only allowed you to take one of your two weeks of vacation time because of a little thing called the "summer rush" which you're pretty sure doesn't really exist, but you've assured your wife you can indeed make it all the way to mid Arizona in less than three days.

While your original plan no doubt included beautiful campgrounds off the beaten path, nestled back in the quiet ancient forests that line the highways of this great nation, you've had to shun that idea for a more practical streamlined approach. No doubt that side trip to Yellowstone was highly overrated anyway, so instead you've opted for a few naps in truck stops along the way.

Has your wife threatened to leave you and head to the spa? Fear not! Happy Camper Campgrounds are here to help.

Yes, Happy Camper Campgrounds combine the convenience of speedy travel with the wonders of nature. No longer will you have to wander far from the expressway; instead, you and your family can simply pull off the pulsing throb of blacktop a mere 100 feet and park it at one of our many luxurious locations. Each campground features 200 RV spots surrounding a man-made lake, complete with refurbished 1980's "retroboats" for paddle boat fun. Imagine the kids taking a dip in the lake while simultaneously waving at passing semi-truck drivers! Yes, the sounds of the freeway make the perfect backdrop for enjoying summer fun.

If swimming isn't in the itinerary, feel free to instead enjoy the complimentary barbecue pit or one of our many stationary charcoal grills. (Sign-up for use is available at the Information Center located in the small building shaped like a duck.) Or befriend one of our many summer residents! Retired couples abound at Happy Camper, making our lodgings their permanent summertime home. Residents such as Viola and Fred of the Sand Lake, Michigan, location are known to feed the children of surprised and unsuspecting parents, taking the worry out of nourishing their offspring in the hurry-scurry that is often necessary in getting the family from Poughkeepsie to San Diego in just five days.

Not yet decided? Here are a few testimonials from previous visitors, taken from their letters without permission:

"Bob and I had to stay at a Happy Camper Campground last summer after we found out the July 4th weekend was already full up at the nearby Lake Wausawgwamamsettie National Forest Campground. Who knew? We weren't sure where we were going to enjoy our 4th weekend, but then my husband remembered whizzing by what looked like a parking lot of RVs. Imagine our surprise when we were able to just drive right off the expressway and start our holiday! The kids played with the chains that hung from the swing set (what a brilliant idea to remove the seats — little Johnny always falls, anyway) and then they collected broken Coke bottles from the side of the expressway. After that, we all roasted marshmallows in one of those bonfires you have set up in old truck tires. The kids were especially excited about the fireworks. We just didn't have the heart to tell them that was the oil refinery across the way. That's our little secret now, isn't it, Happy Camper?"

Or this one from Nell of Cleveland, Ohio:

"After my wife kicked me out last summer, I wasn't sure where I was going to stay. Fortunately, my brother-in-law took pity on me and let me borrow his old Winnebago. I just rolled right down the way, oh, maybe twelve miles from home, which was perfect and outside the limits of my restraining order. After a quick set-up, I met a real sweet gal two trailers down, and we hit it off real nice like. Her name is Fanny, and the minute the divorce is final, me and her, we're gonna get hitched right here in front of the fishin' hole. Now, I know what you're thinkin'. That ain't no fishin' hole, it's the water treatment plant. But me and Fanny, we're not particular. We're just happy we found each other. And yes, we're gonna stay right here in my Winnebago because it's conveniently located across the way from Fanny's job at the all-night adult book and toy emporium."

Have we convinced you yet? Let's just wrap it all up in this one simple statement: You and your family belong here. Now, don't you feel proud?

World News at 6:00

BARRY: I'm Barry Bondsfitch, and this is World News at 6:00. Tonight, we bring you the heartbreaking tale of a woman named Tanya and her trained beluga whale. We have Sylvia Fork live poolside at Tanya Netherfeld's Austin, Texas, home. Sylvia?

Cut to television monitor.

HAL: It's not Sylvia, Barry. It's Hal. Hal McKnight, live from Syria.

BARRY: Sorry, Hal. Let's go to Austin now, and...

HAL: (*forced smile*) No, I'm afraid you won't be going live to Austin. Because I'm in Syria.

BARRY: Well, the story's in Austin, Hal, and weren't you... weren't you fired?

HAL: (*still smiling*) Yes, indeed, Barry. I was fired two months ago, as you well recall, seeing as you were in the staff meeting when it happened. But now I'm in *Syria*, Barry, and *Syria* is where the news is. Not *poolside* in Godforsaken Austin.

BARRY: I'm sure the fine people of (smiling at the camera) Austin would disagree with your assessment of God's harsh judgment, and... (*looks offstage*) why are we not cutting to Sylvia?

HAL: That's because you *can't* cut to Sylvia, Barry. I've hijacked the airwaves.

BARRY: You've hijacked the...

HAL: You bet your sweet patootie. I have hijacked the airwaves, and now we're going to some *real* news here in Syria where things are really heating up. In fact, President Bashar al-Assad...

BARRY: (*interrupting*) How did you even get to Syria, Hal? And where'd you get a cameraman?

HAL: Something called savings, Barry. I *saved* my money, whereas *certain news anchors* have *squandered* their hard earned enchiladas on booze and transgendered *prostitutes*.

BARRY: (*embarrassed*) Those are rumors.

HAL: Really? What color socks are you wearing now, Barry? What color socks?

BARRY: That's none of your business!

HAL: Show the people your socks.

BARRY: I will *not* show the people my socks.

HAL: They're pink, Barry, and they have little hearts on them, am I right? Your lucky evening news socks. I've seen them countless times, as have the entire staff. Let's just be upfront with the people of America. Fess up so that lovely young wife of yours can break free.

BARRY: They're not...

HAL: She's been loyal albeit scorned, and she's stuck by you even though you have been an unfaithful *twit*.

BARRY: What does all this — this

conjecture have to do with Syria? What about Syria? Don't forget the people of...

HAL: Forget Syria! There's unrest! People are downtrodden. But what we need to look at here is the bigger issue.

BARRY: What could be bigger than Syria?

HAL: You tell me, Barry. Beluga whales in Austin? You're the genius behind the whole international department downsizing. 'The world is too serious,' you said. 'We need a lighter approach to the evening news,' you said. You and your fluff pieces And speaking of fluff, let's get back to those socks, shall we?

BARRY: Now, hold on a minute...

HAL: Yes, let's hold on a minute. Let's hold on a minute while I phone your lovely wife

Rachel to let her know what's going on. Just in case she's not watching us right now. Think she's watching us right now, Barry?

BARRY: (*quietly*) Yes. Yes, Boopsie watches every evening. You know that, Hal.

HAL: Indeed, I do. Therefore let me just announce to the entire country — the entire world, really — that I love Rachel. Rachel, honey, I love you. And I'm breaking you free right now, darling.

BARRY: You love my *wife*? *My* wife?

HAL: And darling, as soon as I return from Syria on Tuesday at 8:15, La Guardia, Gate 3C... did you get that? 3C...

BARRY: Now, wait just a cotton pickin' minute, here —

HAL: ...we'll get you that divorce. I have photos, Barry. Right here in my reporter's satchel. Hang on, let me get them.

HAL disappears from view.

BARRY: Oh, no you don't! No, no, no!

HAL: Yes, here they are. Ooo, this first one's a lovely shot of you and Mona Ramona dressed up as Chelsea Handler at the Cabana Room.

HAL begins to turn the photo to the camera.

BARRY: ARRRUGGGHHHH!!!

BARRY jumps up from his news desk and races toward the monitor where HAL is preparing to show the photo. BARRY pushes it over and it crashes. Then he turns to the camera and pulls off his shoes. Just as he's winding up to lob them at the camera, the camera man redirects the camera toward BARRY'S socks, which are indeed pink and covered with hearts. BARRY then winds up and throws the shoes at the camera. The camera blacks out, then cuts to a still shot of an American flag and the sounds of the national anthem.

The Tuesday Salesman

The first time he knocked on her door it was a Tuesday. It was laundry day and she was out back hanging linens. As usual, the knocking provoked a barking fit from the dog, and he ran in circles, performing his special visitor dance around her, which usually concluded with a puddle of dog piss at the feet of the surprised guest.

Martha pushed her hair off her forehead and smoothed out the wrinkles on her apron, a useless task in her estimation. The grime and grit of housecleaning seemed impossible to brush away. She opened the door, saw the salesman, and deflated. The salesman noticed but pretended he didn't. He was used to the unenthusiastic reception.

"Hello, Madame, My name is Bill Crawley. I'd like to introduce to you the world's finest line of floor polishes, created by the legendary cleaning guru himself, Max Maximillian of the Maximillian family fortunes — perhaps you've heard?"

Martha remained deflated but a bit dazed. Shut the door? Throw her Brillo pad at him? She shook her head and listened.

"Well, I'm sure it's only a matter of time now. The Maximillian family is renowned for their inventiveness and forward thinking into the future of cleaning products. They're way ahead of the present 1930's technology. Take, for instance, this bottle of floor polish. Now, most polishes require the woman to apply first, wait for the product to dry (a difficult task with little ones and small dogs about, yes?), then buff and buff to a glowing finish. But Max's

Buffless Polish takes out all the dirty work. You won't have to..." Bill looked down as a warm, wet sensation crept up his left leg and dribbled into his loafer. Ralph looked up at him with glowing pride, another tinkle job well done. Martha noticed too late.

"Oh! Oh, I'm so sorry." She bent down to the dog, who licked the air with glee. "Ralph. Ralphie, what have you done?" She grabbed a dust rag from her pocket and swept at the floor, then Bill's pant leg until she realized what she was doing and stood up, blushing.

Bill laughed it off. He was used to dog pee, cat bites, kid kicks, dirty diapers, and furious housewives who spat on him, then slammed the door before he could remove his hand from the door jamb. "No worries, Mrs..."

"Miss. Miss Harwell." She realized her faux pas and blushed again as Bill's eyes darted to the children's toys on the floor behind her. "Oh," was all she could say.

Bill shook his leg a bit, a sprinkling of urine landing on the hardwood. "If I do say so, Miss Harwell, this would be the perfect opportunity for me to demonstrate the glorious sheen that can be had with Max's Buffless Polish. And perhaps I could..." He held up his damp loafer.

"Of course, of course. Please come in, and I'll get you a towel." She held the door open wider and hoped the children stayed out back so she didn't have to explain later. Martha insisted Bill follow her to the kitchen where she could wipe off his shoe over the sink with a damp cloth.

"This is some mighty impressive linoleum, and I've seen plenty, Miss Harwell."

"Just Martha is fine."

"Martha."

He paused and noticed for the first time that her hair looked quite nice disheveled. Most women didn't appear so spiffy this early in the morning, especially while wearing a dusty house dress and an old ruffled apron. Those were awfully nice ruffles.

She held out her hand and he gave her the loafer. Then he opened up his small carrying case of supplies.

"If you don't mind, I'll just demonstrate here. I'd really love to see the sheen on this

linoleum after Max's Buffless gets a crack at it."
He bent down and set to work on a small spot
near the kitchen table. "You know, the trick to
this stuff is to really — rub it — in." He was used
to this part of the demonstration and never cared
for it, because really, the trick was to buff in the
buffless polish without appearing to be doing any
buffing, and to do it in a way that you were
rubbing it in and back out again quickly, all the
while giving off an appearance of effortlessness.
No huffing allowed.

"That looks like a lot of work, Mr. Crowley."

"Bill, please. Actually, it's quite a breeze
this way." He paused a moment so he didn't lose
his breath. "And just look at the shine!" He was
pleased with his work until he noticed a small
patch of color on his rag that had once been a part
of the linoleum. While he tried to decide between
admitting the problem or moving a chair over it,
Martha had come up from behind him to survey
the results. Her shadow moved over the colorless

bit of linoleum. Bill stood up.

"I'm sincerely sorry, Martha. I've never seen such results before! You know, it does clean remarkably well. Is this floor hand painted, by any chance?"

Martha stared at the spot, stunned. "Oh, this won't do. This will never do." She looked around nervously, as if scared of getting caught. Then she led Bill out of the way and, muttering to herself, started rearranging the chairs in an effort to cover the spot. Bill was about to tell her that's just what he was going to do, but thought better of it.

"I truly am sorry," Bill repeated, "This is — well, this is unacceptable. I'd like to offer you some — how about a free bottle of Max's? No?"

"Let me get you your shoe, Mr. Crawley, and then I think you'd better go now." She handed him his loafer and pushed him through the kitchen and back to the front door, where Bill felt something cold and wet soak through his sock. It was a remarkably large puddle for such a small dog.

"Oh, no. There goes my sock."

Frustrated, Martha mumbled an apology, then pushed Bill and his wet sock out the front door. The door shut, but not in its usual slam. It was more of an "I'm sorry" shut, or so he told himself. He stared at the closed door for a moment or two until it opened back up and his case appeared. Then the door closed again.

Bill limped his way out to the sidewalk and stood staring at the house, waiting for his sock to dry out and wondering who this magnificent creature was behind the door, and why she was Miss, and how many children she had, and who was the Mister who seemed to have her so nervous.

"Hey, Buddy, watch yourself." Someone shoved past him from behind and stared him down, from his loafer to his wet sock, then rested on his case.

"We're not buying anything, so just keep moving through. You salesmen are all alike. Always some new magic hocus pocus. Don't you know there's a depression going on? Soap and water, Sir. Soap and water. Much more economical these days." The man didn't look to be hurting during "these days" and was impeccably dressed in a suit, tie, and hat. He walked up to the house and pushed the door open without knocking.

"Martha, I forgot my briefcase and I'm hungry!" The door slammed shut with a shake.

"Guess that's the Mister," said Bill, and walked away.

The following Tuesday, Bill had a brilliant idea, or at least more brilliant than his usual ideas. He walked up to the door and knocked on it with gusto. This time his hair was more carefully combed and parted, his bow tie had been retied several times over until it was just right, and his loafers were shined and buffed so as to repel liquids.

While Martha did seem surprised to see him there, he was happy to notice she didn't deflate this time.

"Hello, Miss Martha. How do you do? So nice to see you again."

Her eyes looked even bigger than he remembered. Wider. A bit scared, perhaps.

"I was feeling rather poorly about our meeting last week — about the floor, I mean. The meeting was lovely."

Martha looked at the floor, noticed a toy motorcar, and kicked it out of view.

"It was lovely meeting you, too."

"How is the linoleum?"

"Oh, it's just fine. He didn't even notice... I mean, I used the children's paint set. A paint set. And then I put a chair on top of it. You can't even tell, not really, unless the light is on."

"That's fine, that's fine. I'm very relieved to hear that. You see, it's been bothering me, and I wanted to swing by and make you a bit of a gift. I was afraid that — well, that the man of the house might not appreciate such an affront to this sort of high quality linoleum. It really is an excellent grade, one rarely seen these days, and — I suppose it was installed before the depression? Yes? I thought for sure it was.

Nowadays, if anyone even bothers to put in new flooring at all, it's only those horrible asphalt tiles. But, then, who can blame them? The prices." Bill rolled his eyes.

"Yes, the prices."

"Well, I brought you something." He reached down to his case on the porch and opened it.

"Oh! You needn't have gone to any trouble, really."

"None at all. In fact, it's not really — well, it's something, but it's..."

He pulled out a small gleaming ashtray.

"Perhaps you don't smoke, probably you

don't, but I got this at the World's Fair in Chicago awhile back. It's my favorite."

"Then I really mustn't take it, Mr. Crawley."

"Bill. That's alright, I don't smoke. It's just nice to have, you know. For those guests who do."

Somewhere in the background, a door slammed and children began shrieking. The clip of dog nails clattered against the hardwood as Ralph came racing up to the front door, barking and already dribbling. A boy and a girl, twins by the looks of it, ran behind him. The boy was holding a dead mouse and the girl, smudged with dirt, was making the shrill noises only little girls being chased by a boy with a dead mouse can make. They ran in circles around Martha as Ralph continued to puddle up.

In a loud, commanding voice which made Bill jump, Martha ordered them back out the door. "And stay out there, or I'll tell your father about this the instant he walks in the house!" This set the girl to even higher levels of falsetto, but the words seemed to propel them back outside in a hurry, this time through the front door and past Bill, with Ralph barking behind them. The boy stuck his tongue out at Bill before pulling the door shut with a teeth-rattling bang.

"What lovely children you have."

"Yes. Well." Her voice was quiet again. She thought about telling him they weren't really hers, but it seemed much too embarrassing to mention, and explaining was too long and pathetic a process. "Thank you."

"I suppose I'll let you get back to what you were doing. I just wanted to bring you this. Oh!" He realized he was still holding the ashtray, so he handed it to her.

"Thank you ever so much." Bill turned to walk away.

"Um — Bill?"

"Yes?"

"I was just about to sit on the porch here

with some lemonade. Would you care for some? It's rather hot, and I'm sure you must be thirsty, what with all that buffless polishing."

He hadn't polished a single floor all morning, as he had spent most of his time pacing back and forth outside Martha's house with his ashtray, but he didn't want to let on.

"I am rather parched. I'd love some, thank you."

They sat on the front porch for an hour or more, just passing the time and talking about all the sorts of things that usually seem like a waste of breath between two people, but between them, it was more like bearing one's soul. The weather, how prices were so high, why anyone would do something as silly as wearing a raccoon coat in the heat of summer. But no exchange of personal information. Occasionally, this hovered like the elephant on the front porch.

Bill continued to return each Tuesday morning, sometimes with a pretense ("I found this rock and it made me think of you") and sometimes not. When the weather was nice, they sat on the porch and drank lemonade while the children played. When it rained, they sat at the kitchen table and mused over the spot on the floor, wondering how long children's acrylics might last.

Toward the end of September, it was getting too cool for porches and lemonade, so they sat at the kitchen table eating the Bismarck doughnuts that Bill had brought along, and drinking Martha's coffee, which tasted much better than Bill had ever remembered Chock Full O' Nuts tasting. The children were upstairs stomping with passion, so Bill covered his coffee with his hand to keep the flakes of ceiling plaster out of it. Martha had just started in on one of her favorite topics (the woman next door who owned three dachshunds and half a dozen cats) when the front door flew open with a bang, and a man's voice started yelling, "Martha! Hey, Martha!"

Martha jumped up and swore under her

breath. Then she pushed him out the kitchen door and into the laundry line. Bill stood behind a bed sheet and listened through the open window.

"I'm coming, Clinton. One moment!"

Then a man's voice in the kitchen. "Martha, what the hell is all that racket from upstairs? Can't you control those kids? They're like monsters. Hey, a Bismarck."

Bill peeked over the sheet and looked into the kitchen in time to see Clinton shove the rest of Bill's Bismarck into his mouth. It was too bad because Bill loved a good Bismarck.

"These are great! How come you never give me any of these?" asked Clinton around a full mouth, crumbs sprinkling down on his expensive blazer. "Two? Whaddya need two for..." It was then that Clinton noticed that there were not just two Bismarcks, but two cups, two napkins, and two pulled-out kitchen chairs as well. "What the hell? Martha, who's here? Who do you have in my house, and where are they now? It's not that crazy dachshund lady, is it? Her husband? It's her deadbeat husband, I bet! Where is he?"

Clinton leaned over and looked under the kitchen table as if to find a misplaced neighbor. "Damn, woman, what'd you do to my linoleum? This is top quality!" Martha blanched. The light was on, exposing her artwork. "Where'd he go? Out the back door?"

From Bill's position, he could see Martha's face go through a series of transitions. From fear to anger, to firm resolve. She grabbed an iron skillet off the stove and raised it above her head. Bill braced himself for the impact as she brought it down and whacked it with all her might on the kitchen island, an inch from Clinton's hand. Clinton looked like he might win out in a piddle fest against Ralph. His face drained of all color as chunks of the kitchen Formica rained down around them and a large slab of the counter top fell off and clanged to the floor with the skillet. There went more linoleum.

"Clinton!" Martha hollered with all the force in her lungs. "I am not your wife! This isn't fair, and I don't need to take this from you!"

Clinton had never seen Martha like this and he wasn't sure how to react, so he didn't. He just stared at her.

"Those — those monsters upstairs are not even my children."

Bill's ears burned. He felt like he should sneak out the back yard, but he just couldn't leave Martha with that Bismarck muncher.

"I've done everything for you. I've washed your clothes, I've cleaned up after your children, I've taken care of that dribbly dog..."

Clinton found his voice, "But — but you love that dog." Martha thought about that. Yes, she loved the dog. But now was not the time to get sentimental.

"I cook all your meals, Clinton, and I don't have to. I never had to."

"But she was your sister."

"She was my sister and now she's dead. No rule says I have to come in and take care of her lousy husband and her two kids, who, by the way, don't even like me, not one bit. Did you see what Cecil did to me the other day?" She held up her forearm. Bill had wondered about the teeth marks but was afraid to ask.

"Alright, then, how about this?" started Clinton. "How about the fact that you are flat broke and have nowhere to go? How about the fact that I saved your skinny ass from the unemployment line, that you have a roof over your head, a dress —" Martha looked down in amazement at her house dress and gestured to it.

"Not my fault you can't keep the thing clean," said Clinton. "I've kept you housed and fed for three years. You should be thanking me."

"Thanking you? Thanking you? You've humiliated me. Made me feel ashamed of being poor. Here's your thank you." Martha picked up a container of scrubbing powder and threw it at his head. He ducked and it hit the wall behind him, powdering him like a baby's butt.

Then Martha pulled off her apron and threw that at him, too. "And another thing, you lousy little soup slurper. I'm leaving. And I'm taking this ashtray," she pulled the World's Fair ashtray out of the cupboard, "and this salesman's case, and that dog. Come on, Ralphie." Ralph, who was a lousy watchdog except for the fact that when danger was present he watched, came cowering from behind the pie safe.

"What salesman's case? What? So you're just going to run off and become a salesman?"

"No, Clinton, I'm going to run off *with* a salesman."

Clinton stood dumbfounded as Martha went out the kitchen door into the backyard with her ashtray and Bill's case, Ralphie trailing behind. Bill was still standing behind the bed sheet, but now he had a big smile on his face. He didn't even care about the Bismarck.

Martha handed Bill his case and Bill accepted it. Bill handed Martha his arm and she accepted it. Ralph piddled on the bed sheet.

"See you around, Buster," said Bill. He saluted him. "Nice linoleum, but you're a real louse."

"A soup slurper," added Martha.

Then Bill scooped up the dribbling dog and helped Martha hop the fence.

The Parrot

"**A** man walks into a pet shop and says, 'How much for the parrot?'"

"Wait, wait, wait. Stop right there, buddy."

Joe dropped his phone on the floor.

"You... you talk!" he said. The distant "hello hello" sound of his brother came from the receiver on the floor, which went ignored; but his brother was used to it, being the middle child.

"Of course I talk, I'm a parrot," said the parrot. The large gray bird stood in a corner in a sparkling new cage, a remarkably large price tag still dangling from it. "And you paid too much for this cage. Honestly, you humans. You get so caught up in emotionalism over your pets."

Joe stared blankly at the bird, his feet still frozen to the linoleum. He forced his lips to move. "Companions. We call them — you — companions these days."

The parrot chewed thoughtfully on his toe for a moment. "I hear ya. I understand sensitivities to political correctness, but sometimes things go too far. I'm okay with the 'pet' moniker. That's fine. But if I'm gonna be your, what, companion, then there's something we have to clear the air about right now."

"Okay?" It came out more like a question, but then, Joe wasn't very schooled in the fine art of interspecies communication. At least not the sort that involves language.

"You'd better sit down, pal." The parrot grabbed a peanut from his dish and licked at it a bit. "Not bad. Organic? The food is quality, I will say that for you."

"Thanks," said Joe. He sat down on a leather club chair near the bird. Close, but not too close.

"I don't bite. Not usually, anyway." The parrot laughed, a strange mixture of human cackle and bird squawk that levitated Joe's arm hair.

"So... what is it you wanted to talk to me about?" Joe was having a hard time making eye contact. The yellow irises of the bird were punctuated with pupils that grew and shrank rapidly, seeming to focus too much on his face.

"As I was saying, we've gotta set some ground rules here, you and me. You now have a parrot in the house. Congratulations. The monetary commitment is astronomical, no? So you are allowed a few concessions. Number one: I have no problem with you telling chicks that you have me back at your place. I have no problem with you bringing them back here to see me after a long night out dancing. I might even bob my head a little for entertainment purposes. It's kinda cute. See?" Here, the parrot bobbed his head. It was indeed cute. "But if you're gonna do anything, shall we say, nasty, expect that I will imitate any embarrassing noises you make, every chance I get, which is to say whenever your mother or your priest are visiting."

"Uh... okay, I guess so. Not like I have that many female visitors, anyway." Joe sat up. "You think having you here will improve my chances?"

"Most definitely. Okay, Number two: I'll be happy to learn any interesting or witty phrases you might like to teach me, but chances are, I won't feel like saying any of them at all when you have company over. Hiding a tape recorder will not help; I recognize the click. And begging me to say 'Pretty birdie' over and over does nothing for you but make you look like some sort of circus clown. I hate clowns."

"Hate clowns. Got it."

"Great. Take those mental notes; you'll need them. Number three, most important of all: You may not, under any circumstances, tell parrot jokes. Like the one you were about to launch into on the phone right there."

"Really? But they're so much more interesting now that I have you." Joe looked disappointed.

"Yeah, and I'm sure your email inbox is overflowing with parrot jokes from all the friends and family you've told about me. Lemme guess. Most of them end with a dead parrot."

"Well..."

"Or a parrot with a wooden leg, or a parrot in the freezer, or a plucked bird, or a wisecracker with a filthy mouth." The bird paused for a drink of water, tipping his head back so as not to dribble. Then he scratched his head with a claw before giving Joe the stink eye. "Look, you wanted a bird. Let's not be making a holiday out of the whole death thing, okay?"

"Yes. Yes, I think I can do that for you."

"Good. Because I gotta tell you, buster, chances are I'll outlive you. You do realize I've got another 80 years or so on this planet, don't you?"

Joe gripped his knees and calculated food costs and vet bills. "Really? That long?"

"Have you considered an inheritor? It'd

better not be your nephew Bruce. I overheard you talking about him the other day, and he sounds like a feather plucker. I'd suggest you get it together, buddy, and procreate. Raise someone who will take me into the next generation. If you get going now, we can crank out a caretaker for me within the year, maybe two..." At this, he put a toe in his beak and stared thoughtfully at the ceiling. "Yes, two should definitely do it. So you kick the bucket at — how old are you? About 35?"

"Thirty-three. I'm actually not... Yeah, close enough."

"Smoker? Drinker? Gambler? Ladies' man? That's bad for the heart too, you know."

Joe shook his head.

"Good. I'll give you another 40, then. No, 45."

"Uh... thank you. Most generous."

"You're welcome. So that would then put me at a modest 48 or so. I'm prone not to give you an exact age because quite frankly, the guy at the pet store lied to you. No sense ruining that little fantasy. So I'd have another 30 years after your passing, which means you should be thinking arranged marriage for your kid. Get them going early, I say, so I have their offspring to take over in case your kid isn't as fit and healthy as you appear to be. See what I'm saying?"

"Yeah, yeah. But I gotta tell you, I was contemplating staying a bachelor, you know? I got this great apartment, it took me forever to get it and it's only a one-bedroom; I have a nice job and I get to work from home, with you, of course...."

"Yes, that is nice. I really hate to be alone. Flock mentality."

"See? It's a perfect setup. And I was kinda thinking you'd be like my — well, my kid."

Here, the parrot would have raised an eyebrow, had he one to raise. Instead he just leaned forward as if contemplating a good pecking.

"But I can sort of see this arrangement

might be an issue for you. Seeing as you're so worldly. And knowledgeable. I had no idea you'd be so knowledgeable."

"I'm glad to bring that to the table."

"So, well, if we can keep it at that companion stage, I'd be tickled pink to make sure that when I, uh, I buy the farm or kick the bucket or whatever, that you have someone like my cousin Shirley's kid. She's promising. She plays the violin. Very talented."

"Violin. I could go for that. She doesn't even have to be good on the violin. I love annoying sounds." At that, the parrot raised his voice in a cacophonous skreeeee, bobbing his head up and down, neck feathers fluffed to their fullest potential.

Joe held his ears shut and hoped the neighbors below him weren't home. They were sensitive to the noise emanating from his soft soled slippers, so he was sure they weren't going to cotton to this sort of melee.

"Well, that's kinda loud. Nice touch with the feather fluff, though. Yeah, I might just foot the bill for her continued violin lessons. Save us all a hassle, what do you think?"

"All the better, I say."

Joe decided he liked his new friend. The bird wasn't what he'd expected at all. Sure, he knew parrots came with a certain amount of noise, and while the pet store owner had assured him that this gray bird in particular wasn't exactly raucous, he could expect a good deal of talking if Joe were to take the time and have the patience to train the animal properly. But this? This one came fully stocked. He suspected the bird might even have a larger vocabulary than him, which, while unnerving, was kind of nice, too. Perhaps they'd be best friends, hanging out together for his entire life. Maybe he could teach the bird cribbage. Or they could sing duets at parties, astounding all and mostly impressing women, the kind who never paid him any attention, otherwise.

"I recognize that look," said the bird.

"What? What look?" For some reason, Joe felt guilty.

"That look that says, 'Folks, we have a winner. Million dollar parrot right here.' Well, you can knock that off right now. Because truth be told, parrots don't really talk this much."

"Yet there you are."

"Yet here I am. And ain't no one gonna believe that, buddy. I can be as quiet as snow falling on rabbit fur. This here conversing business? That's just between you and me. Got it?"

Barely begotten visions of a night club act whithered from his mind.

"Besides, that's so cliche, don't you think? Man and talking animal hit the circuit? Astound crowds and make man millions while animal barely gets a higher standard of kibble? Nope, not for me. See that window? I can fly right out of it."

"I'm on the eleventh floor. It doesn't even

open."

"Even better."

"Say, you don't play cribbage, do you?"

"Cribbage? Unbelievable. Of all the people in the city... of course I play cribbage. Set me up."

The Fabulous Boyfriend

Dear Mother,

Gerald and I are having a wonderful time on the French Riviera. I really don't know what you were so worried about. He has been nothing but a perfect gentleman the entire time, and he's always watching out for me. Just yesterday after a particularly long and grueling day of shopping for pashminas, Gerald offered to carry my purse. You should have seen him carting it for hours! He was so concerned about me throwing off my spinal alignment that I could hardly get the bag back from him. I thought he would cry, so I let him carry it longer so as to make him feel helpful.

While I could go on and on about our legendary shopping sprees (I have several new pair of strappy sandals, thanks to the generousness of Gerald), there is much bigger news here that I simply cannot wait another moment to share with you. Gerald has proposed! Of course I said yes. I was thrilled and so surprised when he asked. We'd just finished a lazy afternoon in our hotel drinking cosmopolitans and watching old romantic comedies when he pulled out the most lovely diamond ring I'd ever seen. Well, actually I'd seen it before, and maybe you've noticed it before, too. It's that sparkly solitaire he always wears on his pinkie finger. Come to find out, it was his grandmother's and he's been wearing it there all this time in case he got up the nerve to propose. Boy, did he have me fooled. All that talk about it being the perfect match to his diamond stud earring, and I totally fell for that one. Ha ha!

And here you thought he'd never propose! Well, I won't say I told you so because I don't want to make you feel bad or anything. I'm not sure why you had your doubts about Gerald, but I'm sure you'll see him in the same light as I do soon enough. In fact, I'm not supposed to tell you, but he's been buying you presents left and right. Last week I caught him fingering a beautiful silk blouse in a little boutique. It was so expensive and exquisite, and I have to say it rather caught me off guard to see him holding it up to himself in front of a mirror like that. He was telling the store clerk how he'd rather it came in a Prussian blue because it would work with his coloring better, but then he saw me and started laughing so hard he turned red. That man! He's such a joker. Then he pulled out that well-worn American Express and said he just had to get it for you. (Shh! I didn't tell you a thing.)

We've already been discussing the wedding at length, and you can't imagine my surprise when I discovered that Gerald has already put a tremendous amount of thought into it! He even brought along a whole scrapbook that looks like it must have taken years to assemble, although he insists it's just something he threw together before we left for France. Can you believe it? He even has ideas on the centerpieces for the reception and the flowers for the altar. He's thinking something in a ballerina pink and periwinkle theme. What do you think? I'm trying to discourage the pink cummerbunds, but Gerald seems to think this will set the right tone, so of course I'm prone to just let him go with it. He has such an eye for this sort of thing.

How is little Liza doing? Gerald sure misses his dog, and it's so wonderful of you to care for her while we're gone. You don't really have to give her a manicure every week, I hope you know that. Gerald just loves to fuss over her, which is sweet, but sometimes it goes a bit overboard. I mean, I love her too, but I'm not sure I'm ready to give up an entire walk-in closet for her attire. Really, how many tutus does a Pomeranian need? I think she looks best in a simple rhinestone collar, but Gerald feels that leaves her underdressed for most occasions. I guess that's one reason I love him so.

If he cares that much for his dog, you can imagine how he cares for your daughter.

Which reminds me, Gerald has a very close friend (perhaps I've mentioned him before) named Alonzo. Since Gerald is so comfortably set, what with the inheritance and all, he's decided to help Alonzo out because he has come on some rather hard times. So he's hired his dear friend as my personal assistant. Isn't that wonderful? Alonzo will move in with us as soon as we return, and he'll be taking the bedroom right next to ours. I was sort of bothered by this at first. Not by having Alonzo as my assistant, or even by having him move in with us. That will be very handy because he can open those pickle jars, which Gerald never seems to be able to do without hurting his knuckles and squealing. But I was a bit bothered by the idea of having Alonzo in the room right next door. I mean, we'll be newlyweds. I know you're my mother and I certainly don't want to embarrass you, but... I'm not so sure I want another man so close to what may certainly be called the throes of passion. Gerald assures me he won't hear a thing, since the adjoining bathroom is between us. He also insists that if I have a headache or feel a sudden need for privacy, that he can just slip through to Alonzo's room quite easily, where he can sleep on a pullout sofa he'll keep there for just that purpose. But honestly, I don't know when I'd be wanting to kick Gerald out of my bed! As it is, I have a hard enough time keeping him in it. What with his insomnia and all. He's always wandering out after I fall asleep, and he's usually back before I've finished my breakfast in the morning, all smiles and chipper, but he looks so tired, poor thing. We really must have his sleep patterns examined.

Well, I must be off, Mother dear. Gerald promised me a special evening out and I need to get ready. There's some sort of cabaret down the street that he insists I see, although I don't know why. I thought French women were supposed to be so beautiful, but from all the shows he's taken me to so far, I have to say they are mostly a bulky and slightly overdone people. It's all square chins and hard calves around here. And excuse me for saying it, but I've often heard the old chestnuts about French women and shaving, but I always assumed that was in regard to armpits. Not facial hair! Perhaps it's how they feel a woman in show business must appear, but I'd like to see them with a little less makeup. They are somehow quite feminine, though, and I sometimes wonder how I can compete. So I shall do my best and get all dolled up in the new finery my lovely fiance has purchased for me. I'm sure I'll be stiff competition for the ladies at the show when they see what Gerald plans to do with my hair!

Love,

Melanie

Interstate 42 National Museum

We cordially invite you and a guest to the grand opening of the Interstate 95 National Museum! In the spirit of Route 66 and other famous roads nationwide, the Great State of Michigan will officially open its museum doors to the public on July the 20th. But for you and a special guest, we'd like to kick things off with a sneak peak on July the 15th. Three floors of the old Sparkie's Chewing Gum and Caustic Factory will be filled to the brim with mementos and rare treasures, all commemorating Interstate 42, which as you well know, runs from Burnips, Michigan, all the way to Pea Ridge, Arkansas, if you are able to make it through the construction during non-snowy weather (snowy weather being another matter entirely.)

Which leads us to one of the main attractions, a traveling exhibit called "Our

Highways and Byways: Perpetual Construction."
The exhibit will feature a vast array of traffic
cones in various sizes, shapes, and models (our
oldest hailing from 1942), and a photography
exhibit of police shots taken of some of the
country's largest traffic accidents caused by
misplaced construction signage and/or severe road
rage, generally brought on by excess lane closures
during holidays and weekends when no
construction workers were present.

Be sure not to miss the roadkill exhibit on
Level 2, certain to be a big hit with the kiddies. A
special crafts table will be stocked and ready for
your child to recreate their favorite taxidermied
roadkill. (We predict Rocky the Roadster Raccoon
will be a most beloved mascot, what with his
missing tail and his amusingly reconstructed left
flank.) And the kids will really get a kick out of
the pieces-parts room, where they can assemble
collected and preserved animal parts to construct
their own imaginative versions of this country's

great wildlife. (Squir-doe-ssum, anyone?) Of course, don't forget to visit our cafeteria where the kid's menu features 100% organic ground rabbit burgers, lovingly prepared by our cafe short order cook, Al, who is also quite knowledgeable of I-42 history, considering he's lived in a small log cabin 30 feet off the highway for his entire life. (Al provides the meat, and we know not to ask for his secrets!)

Of course, no trip to the museum will be complete without a stop on Level 3 where America's Favorite Billboards are expected to bring in large crowds. See such classics as "John Barnswaggle Wants YOU to Buy a Home in Deepwater! *...ask about our floodplain specials!*" Or who could forget "Marge's Donut Den: Home of Our City's Illustrious Police Force." And then there's this one sure to bring back fond memories: "The Dandelion Festival — Roaring Good Times for Borculo!"

As the curator for the Interstate 42

National Museum, I will strive to bring you the best in highway history. My lifelong goal has been to prove that I-42 has just as much right to international fame and glory as the Route 66 of old. But unlike Route 66, our highway is still in operation. No, it has not failed, this is not a celebration of what's been shut down, and there's a lot less red dirt and pesky tumbleweeds involved, as well as fewer roadrunners, tacky neon signage, and upended Cadillacs planted in the dirt like so many graffiti-clad petunias. We don't showcase cowboy paraphernalia, nor do we cotton to long horned steer, but instead we lean more toward regular cows with black and white on them, who hang at the fence and stare at us with wide-eyed wonder as we yell "mooooo" out our windows. This is the America with which we shall dazzle you. So pile the kids in the car and get on over to the Interstate 42 Museum!

Directions: Take I-42 south from Burnips until you get to the large orange detour signs.

Follow the detour about 30 minutes off the highway until you get to the construction in midtown; in which you must circle around the back parking lot of the Hot Dog Den, then double back until you can get hooked up with the Turner Road detour which should get you on I-42 somewhat after the construction but before the washed-out bridge, so keep your eyes peeled for that one. If you hit the toll road, you've gone too far! Just turn around in the meridian in front of Mary Johnson's double-wide, but don't worry too much about the sign that says "Authorized Vehicles Only." There's hardly ever a cop there. Once you turn back, just follow the signs to the museum and hop off on Exit 80. We're the big old factory with most of the windows still in tact and a large hand painted banner saying, "Welcome Travellors!" (Our art department has yet to answer for that one.)

Dieting Guidelines for Cynthia

That's it! I've had it with my wardrobe of stretch pants and baggy tops. Time to get serious, Cynthia old girl. Gotta set some goals, some guidelines, some unbreakable rules. Bathing suit season is on the horizon, and I can't even stomach getting into shorts, not with this stomach, I can't. Tough love on myself. That's just what I need.

1.) Cold pizza and Coca Cola are not considered breakfast items.

2.) Nor are Fritos. Or cream cheese without the bagel.

3.) Okay, the bagel part isn't such a hot idea, either.

4.) Just because someone leaves half a stale

donut on the counter at work with a sign that says, "Free," this does not mean I am responsible for eating it.

5.) Putting the entire donut in my mouth in one bite, then chewing as fast as possible, washing it down with Janice's abandoned iced tea in the office fridge before anyone spots me, does not mean there's a lower calorie count.

6.) Food prepared by my grandmother is not somehow healthier just because I hide it under one cup of gravy. Even if the gravy is very savory and contains tasty bits of pan scrapings. *Especially* if the gravy is very savory and contains tasty bits of pan scrapings.

7.) Anything purchased from a vendor cart downtown, then eaten while walking, is not healthier just because I am exercising while putting the food into my mouth. Yes, chewing takes more of an effort while walking, hence calories burned must certainly be higher than if I chewed while in a seated position, but... well, okay, maybe if I ate lunch only from vendor carts. Vendor carts that are more than one block from the office. Two blocks. Then I have time to digest the dessert from Lennie's Crepe Carte. Just one, though. Boundaries, Cynthia. Set boundaries.

8.) Do not eat before or after cocktail parties. You always get stung on this one. Just because food will be in small bite-sized pieces and brought only intermittently by tray, does not mean that a full meal must also be consumed before and/or after the party. Think bacon. Think bacon wrapped around cheese. Think bacon wrapped around cheese with a toothpick through it, eaten repeatedly throughout an evening. Think... oh, God. I'm hungry.

9.) Being single is not an excuse for eating

the entire frozen pizza by myself as a bedtime snack. Yes, it seems wasteful and somehow cruel to toss at least half a pizza in the garbage, but I can wrap up the rest and eat some of it for breakfast. No, see Rule #1.

10.) Carrot sticks, carrot sticks, carrot sticks. I cannot stress this enough. Hide them in tiny containers about the house, in all the places I am tempted to snack, i.e. all rooms. Supply ranch dressing. No ranch dressing. No. Bad. I must remember, I overeat because I'm always under pressure. It's the pressure that does it, so relax. Which, come to think of it, could also be caused by undo pressure placed upon myself because of my weight. Yes, I pressure myself way too much. Set the standards too high, and what happens? I shove a Twinkie into my face before you can say Bob's-your-uncle. Maybe I should just lighten up a little. Probably I've put this all on myself, and if I'd cut myself a bit of slack, I bet the pounds would just melt off. I think this calls for a celebratory bit of bacon.

Where Are Our Units?

Dear Mr. Paulson,

Thank you for your recent rental of twelve portable toilets from John's World of Johns. We appreciate your business. However, having only recuperated three of the original twelve units that you borrowed on the eighth of May, I must express our concerns. We do hope you understand that a great deal of late fees have been accrued for the remaining nine units of $27 a day per unit, which is building up rather quickly, as you can imagine. Where are our units, Mr. Paulson?

I do thank you for the three which were returned, or rather, the three that were still at the original location of the drop off. It was our understanding that, upon the conclusion of the Fifth Annual Senior Citizen's Professional Wrestling Festival, all twelve portable toilets would be lined up and awaiting our crew who would then hoist the units onto our truck and take them back to our facility. Imagine our surprise when all we found were three, one being tipped on its side, another having been charred beyond recognition. Our crew searched everywhere, claiming to have even scoured the nearby tree line where, although none of our units were located among the foliage, they did recover half a conference table and a rather frightened 87-year-old woman in a cape.

I must warn you, Mr. Paulson, that wherever these portable toilets are, they are bound to be filled with toxic substances, as you can well imagine, and that they are most likely getting more toxic by the day, this being many months beyond the end of the festivities. My biggest concern is the rumor I hear of a chili eating contest having taken place that very day at the festival. I'm afraid feeding large amounts of chili to men clad in tights and in their golden years is not only unwise but potentially dangerous. We must recuperate those units. I daresay you've suffered at least one small explosion within the last month or so, am I correct? I cannot imagine you want the weight of this on your head. I propose you come forward with the remaining units before someone is injured. This would be a good time for me to tell you that our insurance policy does not cover the accidental explosion of unremitted units.

Let me also inform you that my boss was not very appreciative of the discovery that the two uncharred units appeared to have been restructured somewhat. The addition of spikes to the seat is totally unacceptable and may cause chafing. We also found a fair amount of graffiti within, including several "For a good time call Granny" scribblings, which, when in the pure interest of investigation the numbers were phoned, all rang up at the area's finest retirement homes and assisted living facilities. Upon sanitizing the two units, several items have been recovered, namely: one set of false teeth, several empty prescription bottles of Viagra for a Mr. Larry Flynn (who quite frankly has us all concerned), some sort of Viking hat with horns on it, and an oddly spangled pair of boots, men's size 10. We have retained these items and can return them to you as soon as payment has been made in full, along with a complete explanation as to the whereabouts of our nine missing portable toilets.

Sincerely,
Charles Buck, Jr.
John's World of Johns

Bobo Has a Date

"Speed Dating Tonight! 8:00 to 9:00, first drink free." John hesitated at the sign before he entered the bar. He had never done this before, but it was high time he gave it a try. Dating isn't easy, especially if you're famous. Especially if you're John's kind of famous. Being Bobo the Beagle presented some peculiar dating challenges for John. If his costume for the popular children's show had included a full face mask, things might have been different; instead, his costume consisted of full beagle attire, complete with long floppy ears and a tail that always got in his way during the opening shot jump. But his face was exposed, with nothing but a few glued on whiskers to mask his identity. Fat chance of not being recognized.

In fact, he was recognized all the time. He couldn't, say, shop for produce without a crazed mother asking him to kiss her toddler; he couldn't go to the coffee shop without college girls screaming at him, and not in the way he would have liked. No, they screamed things like, "Omigod, Bobo drinks mochas!" But the high school boys were the worst. It seemed all they wanted to know was whether or not he liked things doggy style.

In actuality, he would have taken things any way they were offered to him; times were tough for John. The last date he could remember ended with what should have been a goodnight kiss; instead, his date suddenly backed away in a fit of laughter. "I'm sorry," she'd said, "I keep thinking you're going to lick me."

He hoped that things would be different with speed dating. The women would have a mere five minutes in subdued lighting in which to recognize him; five minutes that he hoped would reveal his intelligent wit and sparkling conversational skills first. What he hadn't counted on was the first question every woman would ask him: "So, what do you do for a living?"

But that was to come. First, he had to get signed in and get his complimentary adult beverage which he tossed back before even seating himself. As he ordered another, he noticed other men at the bar doing the same thing. A tall, lanky man with bad teeth stood next to him. "First time speed dating?"

"Uh, yes." John mumbled and turned to grab his refill. "Why? Is it obvious?"

"Well, your foot is tapping and you've got a twitch right —" John was afraid Mr. Teeth was going to touch his face. "—right here...ah! There it goes." He took a sip of what appeared to be a Long Island Iced Tea. " There it goes again...hey, is that glue on your face? Or is it snot? Probably it's snot, right?" He guffawed. "Duuuude, you're in for a hot night tonight, I tell ya that right now..." He interrupted himself to slug back more of his drink.

John's hand shot up to his face and he

rubbed. "Glue." Darned whiskers.

"Yeah, dude, whatever." Mr. Teeth laughed again and slapped John on the shoulder before walking away.

"Good luck," he said, making his way to the jukebox.

John finished his second drink and motioned to the bartender for a third. The bartender gave him a look that said, "It'll be alright, really," or at least that's what John hoped it said.

Date #1

At the table, John took extra care in arranging first his beverage and cocktail napkin, then the candle that seemed as if it was too close to the tip of his nose, then the little menu of drink specials. After going through several variations of pretty much the same thing, he finally settled on the first arrangement. He was about to retie his shoes when a man stood up and announced that the speed dating was going to begin. John hadn't even noticed any women, but then, he'd been pretty busy pushing the wrinkles out of his cocktail napkin for awhile. There, lined up around the announcing man were several women, all with tiny notebooks and golf pencils, all with looks on their faces that ranged from, "I'm a contestant on a game show!" to "I am going to vomit." The man instructed the women to take a seat at any of the tables where the men awaited cross examination, and he got stuck right off the bat with "I am going to vomit." The woman didn't look as if she were about to hurl from a fit of nerves, but rather out of some kind of self disgust. She leaned forward and stage whispered to him.

"Don't get any ideas, I'm only here for Chelsea."

"Ladies, ladies," said the announcer, "No talking yet! You must wait for the bell to sound first."

"Chelsea?" John asked.

"Men too, please," the announcer continued. "I know it's all so very exciting, but we really must follow the rules here. Aaaaand go!" Dingdingding! A ship's bell attached to the bar rang repeatedly until John was afraid he'd lose his hearing.

The vomitous woman picked up where they'd left off.

"Yes, Chelsea. That's my very shy, very unfortunate friend over there." She motioned to an uncomfortable looking woman with long strawberry blond hair trying hard to ask Mr. Teeth a question.

"I'm here for moral support and not for a man."

"Oh. Okay. Well, that takes the pressure off some." John fiddled with the straw in his drink. "Would you mind asking me questions, anyway? Perhaps you'd be helping me relax a bit. I'm pretty nervous, you see, and..."

"What do you do for a living?"

"I'm Bobo the Beagle." It flew out. Just like

that, the words flew right out of his mouth and landed on the table between them like a wounded jellyfish. The woman's face froze into position as if she'd just been shot up with an unfortunate amount of Botox.

"Bobo," she stated in disbelief, "Bobo the Beagle. As in, that obnoxious show my niece insists on watching every weekday afternoon. Bobo the Beagle who sings that horrid earworm of a song. The one I wake up to at three in the morning only to find it's lodged itself into my brain and will not allow me respite. That Bobo?"

"I'm afraid that's so."

A painful pause as she took in his features.

"Interesting."

She leaned back in her chair and sipped at her white wine.

"So, Bobo, what do we do now, wait out our five minutes? I've got nothing better to do. Why don't you bring out a sock puppet? Tell me a story."

"There's no need for that, really, no need at all. It's just a job. It's my job. I have a nice home and I drive a luxury vehicle and my shoes cost me $350. But they were on sale because I'm frugal, you see."

"Excellent. Bobo is frugal. That is good to know." She crossed her legs as if to keep him out and signaled to the bartender for another glass of wine. For the next two and a half minutes, she stared at him as he manipulated his cocktail napkin into origami shapes. Then he folded hers into a swan. This was difficult as the napkins were a low grade paper and slightly damp.

As soon as the bell clanged, the woman shot up and headed for another table without even saying goodbye. So far, thought John, this really sucks.

Date #2

The second woman to sit across from him was a bubbly woman who looked too old to be wearing a skirt that short and earrings that large. When she turned her head, which was often, her earrings jangled. She reminded him of an excited puppy who might, without warning, make a tinkle on the floor. She'd brought with her a tall beverage, electric blue in color. It had stained her lips, and he doubted she was aware of that. Now she looked like a frozen puppy.

As soon as the bell dingdingdinged, she was off on a tangent, telling him all about herself and how she was a psychic accountant, and wasn't it great to be at peace with the universe, and he really should try it sometime, she'd balance his checkbook for free, and aren't his shoes stunning! What great leather, but he really ought to try vegan leather instead, his feet would feel great and at peace with nature and cows, especially cows.

"So," she said, mid hair flip, "What do you do for a living?"

John nervously began folding an origami

goat. "I, uh... I'm in show business."

Her eyes lit up. "Oh, my God! You're an actor, right? I knew you were an actor! Lemme guess, lemme guess. You look, omigod, so familiar, I knew the minute I sat down here, but I couldn't place it, lemme think, lemme think." She put her fingers to her temples, closed her eyes, and hummed. "I see... I see fur and, and..." Her eyes squinted tighter before springing open.

"I know, I think I've watched you on t.v. after smoking a spliff! Yeah, I was high, I know it now! I see you on t.v. when I'm high, which is usually, well, pretty much every night, but after cleansing the auras around customer bank statements, so not really night but afternoon maybe fourish, and it's... it's..." Her face fell. "Bobo. Bobo the Beagle."

Why did everyone have to say it like *that*.

"Yes, that's me." He shifted uncomfortably in his chair. "I am Bobo." It felt like a confession.

Her bubbles deflated.

"Oh, my God. So, like, you date... women."

"Yes, usually. Dogs aren't really my thing, it's just... it's a character. A character thing."

She sat back and contemplated him while sucking down more blue beverage. She looked confused, as if he'd just told her the Easter Bunny was a fabrication.

"So, like, how often do you date? I mean, are you allowed to?"

"Allowed to? Of course I'm allowed to. It's not like they keep me in a kennel down at the..."

"No, of course not. I just... I'm surprised. I mean, I see you on there, on that show, and you do that thing with the sock puppets and there's the cartoon segment and story time, and it's just really, really hard to imagine you getting it on, like, with a woman."

"Yeah. Well, there you go."

One and a half minutes of staring at the tabletop, contemplating the candle flame. John swiped a pile of cocktail napkins off a neighboring table and folded one into a panda bear.

"Cute," she said. Then dingdingding, she was gone.

Date #3

The third woman to sit before him was none other than Chelsea. John considered getting up to leave because he couldn't imagine that Chelsea's friend wouldn't have warned her away from the famous man-dog. But she sat down with a shy smile and seemed oblivious to who was across from her. He smiled back. They waited in silence until the ship's bell sounded.

"Hi," Chelsea said.

"Hi."

"Uh, so, what do you do for a living?"

At this point John felt a perceptible shift in his brain. Something altered, something beyond his control, or so he told himself later. It was as if a finger had reached down, nudged and rearranged the contents of his cranium until someone else surfaced. It was him, yes, it was. But him in another form. Perhaps if he'd been born taller and bolder and with stronger ankles.

"Well," he leaned into the table for effect. "I'm with the CIA."

Chelsea's eyes grew large. She leaned forward too.

"Really? The CIA?"

"Yes, I do serious things with serious people. I have a special badge and my car has little buttons inside that, if you push them..." he paused for effect, "things happen." He was thinking that wasn't really a lie. If he pushed the radio button, music came out of the speakers. Not oil slicks. But he really hoped she was imagining oil slicks.

"Like oil slicks?"

He shrugged.

"It's all part of the job. Dangerous stuff." He pointed to the irritated red patch on his face, where he'd scraped the whisker glue off earlier.

"See this?"

"Yeah."

"Acid."

"No!"

"Yes." He rubbed at it pensively. "An Arab prince. Very testy little fellow. But I deflected the brunt of the impact with a... with a spiral notebook. This spot here was much larger at one time, but, thanks to the magic of my personal plastic surgeon, Franz Spurgeon," the name choice made him grimace, but what could he do now? He was on a role. "Franz. He fixed me up, and this is all that is left of the hole that once showed two of my incisors. With my mouth closed."

Chelsea gasped. Then she tipped her head to one side and studied his face.

"Have I seen you before, though, like on the news? 60 Minutes, maybe? Or Maury Povich? I mean, you look familiar."

"Maybe you've been caught up in some intrigue of your own? Perhaps I've had you arrested?"

She shook her head. He liked the way her strawberry blond hair floated like a cloud of cotton candy, except not sticky.

"Detained? Questioned?"

She shook her head again.

"Tortured? I hope to God I haven't had you tortured."

She giggled. "Nope. The last man to torture me was my ex-boyfriend. He stole my puppy. It was a beagle and..." Her eyes lit up.

"Bobo!" She actually sounded excited. "Bobo the Beagle! You're Bobo!"

Cover blown. John was deflated. He wondered how to back pedal out of it, but Chelsea did the footwork for him.

"Don't tell me Bobo works for the CIA! Oh, my goodness!" She raised her hands to her cheeks. "Unbelievable. Bobo the Beagle works for the CIA. What a brilliant cover! Does anyone know this?"

John's new brain gears whirred at a rapid

pace.

"No, of course not. But with my special training, I could tell right away that you were to be trusted. You have the — the eyebrow pattern of a Level One trust factor."

Chelsea beamed.

"My friends do say I'm good at keeping a secret."

"Yes, it shows. And, my life being what it is, it's rather hard to go on without a confidante of some sort. Of course, the Department frowns on it..."

"Of course!" She made a motion as if zipping her lips together.

"But enough about me. Tell me about yourself." He groaned inwardly at this belching of cliche.

"I'm a school teacher. Kindergarten. In fact, I probably see your face every single day at work. You're on backpacks and lunch pails and... but then, you know that already. Umm..." She was getting nervous again. "I'm working on a book. Well, not really a book...yes, it *is* a book. A novel. I write a lot of things, and I've written books before, but nothing worth publishing. This time, though, this time I think I have something." He enjoyed the look in her eyes as she talked about writing. A sense of being lost in herself and happy there.

Dingdingding!

They looked at each other in surprise.

"Was that five minutes? And I didn't even get to ask you about your origami zoo here."

"Oh, that's nothing. You should see my collection at home. It calms the nerves."

The announcer stood up, "Okay everyone, no dilly dallying! You still have six more dates to go, so pull yourselves away," at this he looked at John and Chelsea, "and on to the next table!"

They looked at each other and both mouthed, "Six more?" Then they laughed.

Chelsea grabbed her purse from the back of

her chair. "Well, John, it was wonderful meeting you."

"You too, Chelsea."

She got up hesitantly and began to walk away.

"Chelsea?"

"Yes?"

"I really don't want to go on six more dates."

"Me neither."

"How about we just…"

"Yeah, let's…"

John stood up. The announcer looked at him with the disapproval of a traffic cop, but CIA agents don't get worked up over stuff like that. On their way out the door, Chelsea reached out and grabbed an origami figure. It was a beagle.

The Office Party

Ho ho ho, everyone, and welcome to the fifth annual "Da Bomb" Office Christmas party. Jingle Bells! Hey, Joe, refresh my eggnog, will you, ol' buddy? This stuff makes me feel like a bull at Pamplona, and I'm seeing a red dress over there, whoa Nellie!

I want to thank you all for coming this evening; the party's been a real blast so far and — whoops, there goes my nog! Somebody better clean that up before the conga line gets going. Say, Joe, you better get me a fresh one, eh? Top off the ol' nog, I'm coming in for a landing.

First, let me say that as your fearless leader, your big kahuna, your head cheese, I feel a swell of pride this evening. Just look at you guys — all dressed up for the holidays like that. Wow, especially you, Candice! You're usually so shy, so reserved, so... turtlenecky. But tonight you look scrumptious! What's that you're wearing, cleavage? Beautiful. Just like a high class lady of the evening. Or a news anchor.

I — what is this? The podium? It keeps moving. Someone hold this thing before it gets away.

The buffet is just tremendous, and I appreciate you all bringing a dish to pass this year. That really helped stretch that Christmas party budget, which is great because we were able to afford those lovely decorations at a sizable discount. I just wish it woulda been something more Christmassy, but hey, they sure set a festive and somewhat patriotic mood, what with that firecracker of a spread. Just don't try Bob's special mock seafood salad. We think that's what gave the guys in accounting the trots, and we're very sorry about that. As a rule, don't eat anything with the word "mock" in it and you'll be fine. Just for future reference.

Okay, what've we got here? Christmas

bonuses? Yes, this is usually when I pass out the bonus checks, isn't it? And — Joe, someone seems to have emptied my — thank you.

In lieu of Christmas bonuses this year, I thought we'd try something a little different. I've composed a song and I'm going to sing it to you now. I've brought along my ukulele so's I might serenade you with a lovely ditty. Ed, my ukulele, please. Where's Ed? He's not still hanging out in the supply closet with Janice, is he? If Ed's wife is still around here... oh, there you are, my dear. Maybe you can fetch me my ukulele. Just ask Ed where it is. Supply closet's the second door there on your left. Just past the drinking fountain.

Maybe someone should take that coat rack out of her hand first? Thank you.

In the meantime, I'd like to propose a toast. A toast to all of you, my wonderful employees. As soon as Joe gets this tumbler filled. There we go. I've worked with you all these many years, and you've stuck by me and this company through thick and thin. And thinner. I'll be so very sad, indeed, when I have to spring it on you that we're going under. Oops. Did those words just fall out of my mouth? Gosh, I'm sorry, folks, and here I meant to break the news in song, all peaceful and Kumbaya-like. Probably just the 'nog talking.

HO HO HO! Don't worry, layoffs won't begin until after the New Year, so you can just relax and enjoy the holidays. January second is a long way off yet. Hey, everybody, look on the bright side: You won't be fired till next year! So cheers! I think I'll sit down now. Kumbayah.

Reality Shows That Didn't Make the Cut

Title: Zoo Life

Premise: Contestants are asked to live at the San Francisco Zoo in a cage for the summer. But first they must select a zoo animal to become. To do this, they each don scuba gear and retrieve their "mission" from the bottom of the moray eel exhibit, surfacing before an attack occurs. (This event will be scheduled no sooner than 30 minutes after lunch). For example, Phyllis from Kalamazoo may be required to become the zoo's new wildebeest. She will then be led to her cage and fed a steady diet of various Savannah grasses, and here she will remain until one of the zoo's summertime visitors can guess her species and properly spell it in Latin.

Title: The Potato Wars

Premise: In the spirit of the world's best

competitive cooking shows, chefs representing a variety of cuisines will be given a 40-pound bag of spuds, some butter, and a mixer with which to create a large tower of mashed or au gratin potatoes in 20 minutes or less. (Any additional spices or decorative bits must be supplied by the contestants. Sharp, pointy things are highly dangerous in such a competition, thus encouraged.) Whoever is able to create the most intricate and tasty pile will be given the opportunity to shove their nemesis into their creation at the end of the show. The winner will receive an all-expenses-paid trip to the Potato Famine & Dirt Mound Museum in Dublin, Ireland, where they will be honored with a plaque and a bronzed russet.

Title: Barstool Dash

Premise: Everyone loves a good barstool. But a motorized barstool takes things to a whole new level of excitement. Envision contestants bound to their very own Stoolie 1300 Motorized Barstool, where they will be required to tootle around New York City for 48 hours straight, collecting money in a tin can to raise funds for much needed barstool research. The first contestant to make it to Time's Square with $1,000 in quarters will win a night on the town with the King of Grass himself, Willie Nelson, a longtime connoisseur of barstools. The show will conclude with Mr. Nelson serenading the winner, then smashing the motorized barstool with his guitar.

Title: The Lobster of Death

Premise: Based on Japanese game shows where contestants are led through harrowing physical challenges, The Lobster of Death heightens the play. If you can handle running a gauntlet filled with raging proboscis monkeys, wading through a vat of Greek style yogurt (fruit on the bottom), then scaling a rope wall to reach a platform 20 feet above the audience where the lobster of death awaits you, then buckle on your boots and prepare to play. The winner will have hoisted the furious lobster above his or her head while singing the show's theme song before hurling the giant crustacean into a cauldron of boiling water. Prize for winning: $1,000 in cash, a gallon of drawn butter, and two tickets to Cirque du Soleil.

Title: Mob House

Premise: For this thrilling reality show, ten beautiful people between the ages of 19 and 20 will be asked to live together in a gaudy pseudo-mansion in the suburbs where they will be required to form their own actual ring of organized crime. Hosted by one incognito member of the Gambino family, each team of five will be given their very own waste management company and will oversee three blocks of downtown streets where they will gather money from local vendors.

As funds are collected and thus stored safely away in the attics and crawlspaces of neighboring homes (unbeknownst to the owners, of course) teams will win prizes for goals achieved; e.g., the first team to reach the 10K mark will receive a get-out-of-jail-free card and an El Camino. The winning team will have successfully overthrown the opposing "family" of contestants, while gaining respect and avoiding suspicion of tax evasion.

Title: Stunt Man

Premise: Disgruntled employees from across the spectrum will be brought in to compete in the exciting, challenging world of movie stunts. With little preparation, training, or knee pads, the newly released "stunt men" will be asked to attempt dangerous and death defying tricks for the very best of the Hollywood B movies being filmed today. Scant guidance will be provided by our very own Crush Stevenson, an 85-year-old veteran of the stunt industry. While he may be hard of hearing and blind in one eye, his advice is stellar and his guidance remarkable. He'll give contestants sage advice on stop, drop, and roll "help I'm on fire" procedures, as well as the "pull" command shouted from the ground as newbies parachute off the Hollywood sign. The winner will bankroll a whopping $10,000 in life insurance. Losers will return to their previously unexciting and unfulfilling lives, left to ponder what might have been.

Moving Day

Any day you get sent home early from work for reasons that are not your fault is a good day. Today is one of those. The Internet went down thanks to a beehive within the cable box outside, so my work has been suspended until further notice. My boss thinks it'll be tomorrow. But if the cable guy is on my side just this once, he won't show up to fix it for a few more days.

I walk back to my apartment, soaking up the sun and drinking the last of a celebratory coffee. Maybe I'll read a book on my balcony until dusk, then meet up with Susan at that Thai place we've both been wanting to try. Loose, rambly thoughts flit through my cerebral space until the sight of a moving van jolts me out of my zone. Moving vans are rather commonplace outside an apartment building, and they always mean noise: men yelling up and down the stairwells, boxes and furniture bumping against the walls, the wails of the moving family as a precious China figurine from great grandma careens down a hallway and smashes, a grumbled oops from a barely regretful man in overalls. They have insurance, and they like to make use of it.

I sigh. Maybe it won't be so bad. Maybe they're almost done here. The truck does look about half full with boxes, and the television is already being loaded up. Same kind as mine. I mentally scan through my neighbors, trying to guess who's flying the coop. The guy in 1B? He hates it here. It's probably him. Then again, we all sort of hate it here. Management is terrible.

I climb the stairs to my second-floor unit and am stunned when I reach the top. My apartment door is open! I approach stealthily and peer around the corner. My heart bangs out against my chest and my stomach retreats for my shoes. My fully decorated apartment, my clean, organized haven of peace is almost empty! I lean against the door jamb with my mouth agape and ready to accept flies from the neighbor's ever present garbage bag in the hallway. A mover whisks past me and enters my apartment, heading straight for my bedroom.

"Excuse me," I squeak, an intruder in my own space. "Excuse me, what's going on here?"

"What's going on here?" he echoes. "We're moving, lady. You can't be in here."

"But I live here." I enter the living room and do a 360, taking in the bare walls and the stack of empty boxes in the corner.

"Why didn't you say so?" The man comes back out of my bedroom, carrying an armload of my Hello Kitty stuffed animal collection. "We've been wondering where you were." He dumps the toys in a box with no ceremony, and I cringe when he stuffs them down with one of his big paws before taping the box shut. Maybe they can't breathe in there.

"But I'm not moving. I live here. I mean,

I'm still living here."

"Nope. Today's your moving day. Got it right here." He moves to my kitchen counter and grabs his clipboard. "2C. That's you." He points to my open front door and its tarnished brass 2C.

"Yes, but I'm not moving."

"Yes you are."

"No I'm not."

"Yes you are."

Obviously, this is getting nowhere. I grab for the box of Hello Kitty dolls and begin to walk back to my bedroom. The mover grabs the box and tries to pull it away, but I've got a good hold on it. "These are mine! My kitties!" I yank hard and he loses his grip; between the two of us, the cardboard has smashed and kitties spill everywhere. I scoop up an armful, but he's down on the floor scooping faster and shoving them back into the broken box.

"Look, lady, obviously you're having issues with the whole moving thing." Stuff, stuff. "It happens, okay? I understand. I see this every day, people freakin' out over leaving the place they call home, but you're gonna have to get over it." He finishes stuffing the box and slams it into the corner. I'm sitting on the floor still holding one kitty, the one dressed as a bunny in pink ears. I hug it to me and stare at him in disbelief. This cannot be happening.

Another man tromps into the apartment, his dirty work boots leaving a trail behind him. I just vacuumed yesterday.

"Hey," he says to the first mover, "we gotta get a move on and get this stuff on the road before noon, or we won't get any traction."

"Where... where are we going?" I ask.

"Albuquerque," says mover number one, with a hint of compassion. He thinks I'm shattered. I toss the bunny.

"*Albuquerque*? I'm moving to Albuquerque? Says who?"

He waves the clipboard at me. "Says the

main office! Look, I get the tear-off sheet in the morning, I get my ass into that truck out there, and I hightail it to the building *and* the apartment number as indicated on the sheet. My crew works hard to get all this stuff packed up and in the truck, then I gotta get me in that truck with Hal, who, by the way, has a perpetual case of flatulence and is no picnic to travel with, and I gotta drive with that nut job for 3,000 miles to get your shit to your new place. You are not making this easy on me!"

"I am not moving to Albuquerque!"

"Oh, yes you are!"

Two more men walk into the apartment and head for the kitchen. I hear my collection of Le Creuset being boxed up, then I hear the flatware drawer being dumped on top of them. They walk by me with the boxes as I shout.

"I don't even know where Albuquerque is! I've never been there, it's a desert wasteland according to the Travel Channel, and I'm pretty sure there are snakes. Have you even seen Breaking Bad? I am *not* moving. End of story. So grab your... your stupid clipboard and shove it up your... your *butt* and get out of my apartment. This is my day off! My unofficial, don't-look-a-gift-horse-in-the-mouth, day off!"

Movers come back in and take more of my stuff out, all while I wave the clipboard at the man. His eyes soften at my distress, and he carefully approaches me as if I'm a scared rabbit in need of rescue. Taking my elbow, he leads me out to the hallway and down the stairs. "Fresh air," he says, and pulls me off to the side where we sit down on a top step away from the continuous traffic of my stuff heading for a van I did not hire.

"You got a job here?" he asks.

"Yeah. Yeah, I got a job here." I'm breathing hard and feel an anxiety attack forming in my chest. He rests his hand on my shoulder, tentatively at first, then pats me on the head like I'm five.

"You like it?"

"Not particularly." I gulp big breaths of air and watch my antique dresser float by. "It's tough sometimes, you know? They expect a lot of me there, but it's my job. I've been there for nine years!"

"Wow, that's a long time." He stares out at the truck and leans back on his hands. "What do you do there?"

"Computer. Data. I sit there mostly, staring at the screen. It's not glamorous, but hey, it's a paycheck, even if I never get a raise. And it's what I'm trained to do, so I do it."

"Yeah, well..."

Two men come out of the building clutching armloads of my clothing, hangers dangling. Up ramp, into truck.

"What do you really want to do? I mean, if you could do anything at all, no consequences, no worries about money, what would you do with your life?"

"I'd paint." It is said without hesitation. I didn't know that was coming. "I used to paint all the time, and it's what I really love to do, but I doubt I've got the talent for that."

"Oh, sure you do!" He sits up. "I packed your paintings a couple hours ago, and they're stunning!"

"Really?"

"Yeah, I love that one, that sort of..." he searches for words with his hands, "that one with the red and gold where it sorta looks like a sun but you're not sure?"

"That's the sun! Yes, that's exactly what I was going for!"

"See? You got talent. And I should know. My brother-in-law's an art dealer in Boise. I seen his gallery at least a dozen times. Plus sometimes they give me small pieces for Christmas and such, little impressionistic ones for the front hall. It's a small place I got, but it's got art so it's all good."

"Yeah? Wow." My heart is thumping now,

but for different reasons.

"You know, there's quite the art community in Albuquerque. Santa Fe, Taos, and all that."

"Really?" I watch the last of my wardrobe go by and ponder the sheer mass of items I never wear. Two men are lugging a large trunk of my sweaters, and I wonder if I'd need them in the desert. "There go my sweaters."

"Keep those. The nights are cool. And they still got a winter, but it's better than here. I'll be jealous of you come January. Real jealous."

"I suppose I could go... I mean, I have a few days off probably, so I could check it out, you know?"

"Sure! Sure you can, kid. Check the place out, see how you acclimate. And hey, it looks like your stuff is headed for a decent neighborhood. A two-bedroom on the northeast end, and I bet it's got a view of the mountains."

"Mountains." I think about my paint brushes, the smell of turpentine, the feel of a stretched canvas and the joy of setting up my easel. Paint on my hands. Ruined shirts that look so much better with splotches of color smeared on the sleeves. I stand up, decided. The mover stands up too, dusts off his hands, and follows me back into the building.

From the top of the stairs, there's a loud crash and the sound of shattering pottery, followed by a string of expletives. "Hey, boss!"

"What'd you break?"

"Some urn thingie with a lot of dust in it. Sorry."

"That's okay," I shout up the stairwell, "Grandma would've hated the desert."

Reservations

It is my job as a reservations desk clerk in the swanky downtown Le Veau d'Or Hotel to bend over backwards in order to please each and every rich, pampered, spoiled guest. In other words, I am paid a small sum to kiss ass.

Perhaps you think I'd be bitter, but I am not. It is the job I have chosen, or rather the job I am stuck with at present, and it works for now. At least until I get my screenplay into the well manicured hands of a visiting Hollywood director. I plan to secret it into his room service tray this evening, complete with extra pillow mints. Just to soften him up.

Most days, it's the same thing over and over again. A guest walks up to my counter, demands the best room we have, insists on a view, extra soaps, maybe an afternoon at our in-house spa with Hans who makes me sick because he's twice as broad through the shoulders as I am, and if I'm lucky, the guest slips me a twenty or a fifty, even a hundred, in order to be assured I owe them big time.

But on one day not so long ago, a spindly little weasel man came up to the counter and handed me his card. Turns out he was the personal assistant to Ms. Myrna Gonzalez. Yes, that Ms. Myrna. You know her music, that thumpitty stuff you hear in clubs all the time, the kind that gets repeated on the radio six times an hour, the kind that starts out so hip it's passe by the next morning, the instrumental version playing in your dentist's office by next week. If you've ever been privy to one of Ms. Myrna's television interviews, or if you've ever picked up a magazine or surfed the net, then you know of her notorious reputation for being a demanding and impossible human being. I am here to tell you that everything you hear is absolutely true. And I've never met her.

So, anyway, there's weasel man standing before me, looking like he hasn't had a proper bowel movement in about eight days. He says the tour bus is outside, and Ms. Myrna wants a room pronto because she's sick of sleeping in a tour bus and requires emergency spa treatments, along with a case of chilled Moroccan mineral water and fresh squeezed pomegranate juice so she can properly hydrate for tomorrow evening's concert. He's fidgeting with my bell, which I hate. I don't like having that bell there to begin with, but rules are rules. I usually keep it back far enough to discourage the wealthy kiddies from ringing it and shouting, "Hey, boy, I need some service here." Unfortunately, weasel man is short, but not that short. He can just reach it, and he's tinking the thing over and over again out of sheer nervous energy.

"Ms. Myrna is in great distress," he tells me. "She'll require a room immediately, and she'd like one overlooking the park."

"What park?" I ask. We are smack downtown. The closest we have to overlooking a park is the view of 48th Street rush hour.

"I don't know what park, but that's what she wants. Can't you do something about that?"

I'm pretty sure he's going to have an aneurysm right here on the lobby floor.

"I'll have someone look into it." I type away on my computer, slamming in all sorts of code words for "crazy guest," and "weasel man."

"Also," he fidgets so hard on the bell it slides over the counter and onto the floor — on my side — so I leave it there, "she'll need an adjoining room."

"Certainly, sir. Is that for you?"

His eyes bug out. "For me? Surely you jest. I'll stay on the tour bus. No, the adjoining room is required for her chickens."

"Chickens, sir?"

"Yes, Ms. Myrna never goes anywhere without her six chickens."

"Six chickens, sir?"

"Three of them can't walk very well, so ramps are needed in order to reach the bed."

I don't ask, but my face must betray my desire for further explanation.

"They're factory farm rescues. She made me go in there," here he quivers, "and...and sneak in and... and I had to grab as many as I could before they caught me. It was horrible. The stench! I had to burn all my clothing as well as my hair."

"I'm sorry to hear that, sir." I typed more into the computer. "Chickens. Ramp. Handicap accommodations."

"Yes, thank you. And Ms. Myrna also requests that her tub be filled with fine French green clay."

Here, I stop typing. Chickens are one thing, but if I have a tub filled with clay, the housekeeping department will never forgive me. I stare hard at weasel man, hoping for a break here. But no dice. He shakes his head vehemently.

"We really need that clay. I have the number of a source, and you can give them a call and they'll fly it in immediately. She'll want it for her six o'clock bathing regimen." He scribbles a name and number of the clay supplier on the back of his business card. 'Crasse Cher' located in L.A. Of course.

While Ms. Myrna no doubt waited impatiently in her chariot blocking the valet parking drive, weasel man and I hashed out the great need for fresh chicken salad (the irony hurts, doesn't it?), organic mung sprouts, and the implementation of her own handwoven organic Egyptian cotton sheets in place of our own unsatisfactory $300-a-flat-sheet bedding.

Finally, the credit card was handed over and I was able to begin the process of getting them signed in.

"Wait! I almost forgot! How are your towels here?"

"Towels? They're fine. They're excellent, in

fact. We use a special Italian towel that is famous the world over for its loft and tightness of weave." This, of course, was all bullpucky. They are indeed fine towels, don't get me wrong, but they could just as well have come from Cambodia, for all I know. I make a mental note to have all the tags cut off.

"May I see one, please?"

"A towel? You want to see a towel?"

"Yes, please. Please. My job is on the line here."

"You mean she doesn't travel with her own special towels?"

"She claims hotel housekeeping steals them."

"Well, in that case..." I speed off to find a linen cart in a nearby hallway, and I pick up one of our extra large bath towels. Then I carry it in my best 'footman to the king' impersonation before laying it before the assistant with a flourish.

He fingers it. He scrutinizes. He pulls a corner of the towel close to his eyes and begins to count the little terrycloth loops. Then he lets go of the fabric, deflated.

"I'm sorry. This just won't do."

"Sir?"

"These towels aren't nearly fluffy enough. We'll have to go elsewhere."

"But the French clay. The mineral water. The... dear Lord, the chickens."

He shakes his head. "We almost had it but for the towels." With that, he whisks the credit card from the counter and turns on his heel. Before heading out the door, he pauses, then turns back.

"Here," he says, and lays something on the counter. Two tickets to Ms. Myrna's show for tomorrow night. Front row.

For some reason — perhaps it was the chickens, I don't know — I'm not up for it. But I bet the tickets will look great on that service tray next to my screenplay.

The Beginning and Ending of Bob

Bob brushed his teeth with vigor for the fourth time that morning. He must be absolutely certain the DNA in his mouth were sparkling clean. Today, Bob had a mission. He pulled a brochure from the pocket of his terrycloth robe, leaving a sudsy toothbrush to hang from his mouth. The brochure, emblazoned with the title "You and Your Other You," was dog-eared from much reading. He took one look at the brochure and slapped it down on the bathroom counter. "Hot diggity dog! Today's the day, Bob!" His toothpaste splattered on the mirror, creating a Jackson Pollack of his enthusiasm. Today, Bob was being cloned.

Bob was a thirty-something man with thinning brown hair. A bachelor who always longed for children, he'd been unable to find a suitable wife or an egg bank. Bob decided to take matters into his own hands after he found the brochure left behind on the bus seat. The perfect solution! Bob always rather liked himself and enjoyed his own company, so why not have a clone made of himself that he could raise from infancy? Mother always said that Bob was a good baby, so he knew there'd be no colicky behavior. Plus, he'd finally have someone who would enjoy his Coke bottle collection. No one else took much interest in it; but another him, now, that was another thing entirely.

After Bob had his DNA sample taken from the inside of his mouth with a Q-tip, he had to wait for the incubation period. Then, he was allowed to come in once a week to view his little self, safe and snug, from petri dish to test tube to really big test tube, until finally the day came for them to pour Little Bob from his large glass. Oh, never had Big Bob felt such a feeling! Here right in his arms was — well, himself! Finally, someone would truly understand him and love him. He looked forward to all the years they would spend together, both of them hating cooked spinach and loving reruns of Friends and Seinfeld.

But first, better sleeping arrangements had to be made. You see, Little Bob wasn't used to the cushy feeling of an ordinary crib. Big Bob finally realized that what Little Bob needed was a very large petri dish, so he bought the largest casserole pan he could find. And as Little Bob grew bigger, he needed to adjust the situation accordingly. By the time Little Bob was two, he slept in the bathtub each night. This disappointed Big Bob, since he himself preferred the comfort of a goose down pillow and a therapeutic mattress pad. Big Bob was beginning to realize that his little self did not necessarily like everything he did.

Another large disappointment came when Little Bob was 12 and Big Bob discovered that the boy did not really enjoy the Coke bottle collection. It was beyond Little Bob's understanding why anyone would want to save all those odd glass bottles. He had never seen them in the store, and they looked kind of archaic to his hip young eyes. It seemed to make much more sense to just get the plastic ones or the cans and get his ten cent deposit back afterward. Little Bob preferred his collection of Hexbugs to that of Coca-Cola memorabilia. After all, with a Hexbug, there was something to do with it. You could have battles or just run it around in an effort to scare the cat. The bottles just sat there all dusty. Big Bob figured that maybe he enjoyed the bottles because they reminded him of his childhood, at least the first childhood of Bob the Original. He tried serving Coke to Little Bob in the bottles, but to no avail. Little Bob found the bottles much too heavy and cumbersome. He preferred the plastic.

Eventually, Little Bob got bigger than Big Bob. Little Bob's diet was much healthier than Big Bob's had ever been. Big Bob grew up on peanut butter and jelly, a bag of potato chips, and a Twinkie for lunch. When he was 12, no one knew smoking was bad for your health. He always figured that he got into trouble for smoking cigarettes behind the garage because smoking was impolite for a 12-year-old, plus his mother said he was trying to grow up too fast. In actuality, the cigarettes stunted Bob's growth, so his mom missed the boat on that one.

When Little Bob was a teenager, he began the habit of slathering himself with SPF 30 before going out into the sun. Big Bob had loved the sun as a youngster, and he couldn't imagine his childhood without the first burn and peel of the summer. But Little Bob warned against the dangerous rays of the sun. He knew because he had an environment class in high school. Big Bob took things like math and history in school. Not environmental studies.

But they did have a few things in common, the Bobs. For instance, they looked a lot alike. Except for Little Bob's stature and better muscle tone, he looked just like Big Bob did at his age. They had the same hair and eyes, but Little Bob's voice was slightly lower, while Big Bob's was scratchier due to the years of smoking. And they did both hate spinach. Big Bob was pleased about that. The other thing, the most important thing that they had in common was the fact that they really liked each other, enjoyed one another's company. They had the same sense of humor, although Little Bob's was a bit more refined due to all those college classes Big Bob never got around to. Sometimes it made Big Bob feel inferior and self conscious, but mostly it just made him proud. Looking at himself from a distance like this, he realized he was a lot smarter than he gave himself credit for. Maybe if he'd just applied himself more in school. But then, he had the second time around.

Little Bob graduated college with honors and went on to medical school. And throughout all his years of higher learning, he called Big Bob at least twice weekly to let him know how he was doing. By this time, Big Bob was considering retirement from his years at the post office. He was getting tired of working the front counter every day, counting out stamps and handing out Priority Mail boxes he knew most people were just using as free moving material. Besides, he'd been giving it a lot of thought. Little Bob's success in medical school had instilled in him a new sense of confidence, almost entitlement. He knew he was smart, knew he could do a lot better than this. Perhaps he'd take his retirement fund and travel, or finally write that book he'd been putting off all these years. Little Bob was nothing but supportive. He said he, too, felt the call of the written word, but now that he was up to his elbows in people's internal organs (he was going into surgery), he didn't see how he'd have the time to do that quite yet. But if Big Bob did, then he'd know he at least had a shot at it himself someday.

As hard as it was to leave the home that the Bobs had shared together, Big Bob packed everything up and headed to Venice, which, he discovered, is damp. The climate gave his sinuses a bit of trouble, but he managed to rent a small place overlooking much water and gondolas and shouting Italians, and he wrote. The only things that ever interrupted his writing were fresh bread and pasta breaks and the occasional visit from Little Bob, who was now a full fledged surgeon. And even though his specialty was intestinal related, he did give Big Bob advice and pills for the sinusitis. They'd sit in little Italian restaurants together and eat their pasta, identical twirling motions, identical flips of napkins and sips of lusty red wines. And they both endured identical hangovers when they imbibed too much limoncello.

The last time Little Bob visited Big Bob in Venice was right after the book was finished and had been accepted by a publisher. Big Bob was beside himself with glee and couldn't wait to share this momentous occasion with Little Bob. But Bob the younger had a big surprise for Bob the older.

This time, he'd brought Janice.

It had never occurred to Big Bob that a younger version of himself would actually find a woman who would accept and love him, but there before him was the vision that was Janice. Sure, her nose was a little unusual; some might even use the word 'bulbous'. But that didn't bother him in the least. He had a thing for unusual noses; seems his younger self did, too.

The first night they were in Venice, they all went out to dinner at the Bobs' favorite spot. The moon hung low and large over the outdoor patio, and an elderly gentleman with an accordion swung around making faces that would look like romance on a younger man, but on him, it looked more like pain.

After a bottle of wine and then two, the sounds of Janice's laughter were getting lodged deep into the brain of Big Bob. For the first time in his life he found himself hopelessly and inexplicably in love. In fact, the depth and breadth of his love for her was only to be matched by the love emanating from Little Bob's wine-filled eyes.

Janice appeared to be having the time of her life, and stated that she'd never had so much fun with two such charming men. She couldn't believe how alike father and son were; son had never revealed the secret to their alikeness, had no intention of doing so. Perhaps if he had, he would have made things a bit easier on Janice who could not find an explanation for why she was having such intense feelings for both men.

For Bob the Younger, she felt all that first-time love mixed with infatuation and physical attraction. But for Bob the Older, there was something very different. While the physical attraction was not so intense, she felt more drawn to what she found there in his eyes; the intelligence of Little Bob was indeed in Big Bob's eyes, but there was also something more mellow, more wise, and more... more like home.

Over the next two weeks, the three of them

spent much time together, traveling about Italy so Big Bob could finally explore the country he now considered his home. On the one hand, he couldn't be happier. He had Little Bob at his side; he had found true love for the first time in his life; but so had Little Bob. The combination of pain and joy were excruciating. Janice, too, shared in this horrible jumble of emotion. Little Bob remained oblivious and enjoyed his vacation all the more, knowing that on their last night in Italy he planned on proposing to Janice.

When that night finally arrived, the trio were back in Venice. Little Bob took Janice out on a gondola ride, just the two of them, while Big Bob sat back at his apartment contemplating life, the universe, and swimming helplessly after gondolas. When Little Bob and Janice returned, Janice was wearing a diamond ring on her left hand. They broke the news to Big Bob. Big Bob's stomach dropped and ricocheted off his colon. Janice's eyes betrayed confusion, which Little Bob was too joyous to notice. After briefly considering flinging himself off the balcony and into the water, Big Bob congratulated the young couple and hugged Janice. When he hugged her, he felt it. He felt that she loved him just as intensely as he loved her. The hug was too tight, too long. He looked her deep in the eyes and knew they were saying goodbye to one another.

The next day, he drove the couple to the airport, Little Bob chatting away about buying them a big home as soon as his residency was done. He couldn't wait for Big Bob to make the trip back stateside for his book tour so he could stay with them, perhaps take a tour of the hospital. Big Bob said yes, that would be nice, and I'll be so happy to see you both again, won't that be wonderful. But his eyes said he wouldn't be coming back, and Janice knew it.

Big Bob stayed at the airport until the plane took off; he watched it from the observatory deck and cried. He wasn't worried about Little

Bob because he had Janice. And he wasn't worried about Janice, because even though she had just left the love of her life, she'd left him with the love of her life.

Weeks passed, then months. The book came out in hardcover and was a huge success, even though Bob had to cancel his book tour in the States. Instead, he hung around the apartment and spent time looking at old photographs. Little Bob in his test tube; as a toddler asleep in the bathtub; his first day of school, a lunch bag no doubt filled with tofu sandwiches and nori rolls at his side.

Little Bob called often, wondering when they could expect him for a visit. The wedding was soon, he said, and they couldn't wait to see him. It was to be a small affair, just a quick ceremony, but if he could join them as witness, they would be thrilled. It was hard to turn them down, but he feigned an illness; dengue fever, he said, which, while not a logical choice of illnesses, it wasn't something one wanted to travel with. Yes, dengue. It's quite a problem in Venice these days, what with the moisture. Little Bob was disappointed but understood somehow, thinking to himself that if the situation were reversed, he, too, would probably contract a case of dengue, if not a good whopping dose of typhoid.

Then, it happened. Several months after the wedding, Little Bob called with the news: Janice was pregnant. At first, Bob had mixed feelings. He was happy for Little Bob, knew he'd make a great dad. And Janice would no doubt make a beautiful, kind, and affectionate mother. But it plunked one more brick in the wall between him and Janice.

Or did it?

That night, as Bob rowed himself through the streets of Venice, a loaf of bread and a bottle of wine tucked between his knees, it occurred to him that not only was the baby Janice was carrying Little Bob's; it was his. Janice was carrying his baby. The proof was in the DNA. And while he was never able to join with her the way two people in love would want to do, and while he'd never see her again, she was indeed pregnant with his child, carried a bit of himself within her, would raise their son or daughter. He wished she knew that, wished she understood that the child belonged in part to both the men she loved, but it would have to be enough that he knew it himself.

He slipped the oars into the water and pulled, the slooshing sound a comfort. Off in the distance, some Italians yelled at each other. Something about love. Amore. And faithfulness. He could do that. He would give her that.

A Hangover for All Seasons

There is something about one's thirtieth birthday that can curdle the very soul; at least, this was my case. Twenty-nine was blissfully ignorant of the thirty to come, and so when the hallowed day did arrive, I thought to plunge myself into the Seine and to my certain death. But, as luck would have it, I live in Kalamazoo, the river of which would hardly be fitting for a poetic end. A comically twisted neck, perhaps; maybe followed up by a short stay in a mental facility. But death would be tricked and I'd still be looking at the backside of thirty.

My friends, what few I have, thought it was fit to take me out for my birthday, something I tried in vain to prevent, but they were having none of it. "We must celebrate!" they said. "We'll buy you adult beverages that glow!" they said. "We'll humiliate you in public and make the waitstaff sing demeaning ditties to you in front of a crowd of strangers while you wear a silly hat," they said. I may have imagined that last part, but that's how these things generally go. If I were to be forced into turning thirty, I'd much prefer to do it at home with a baked frozen lasagna, a bottle of red wine all to myself, and approximately three bad DVDs the likes of which would allow for a blissful slumber commencing sometime before 10:00. This was not to be. Can no one have the birthday they choose?

We arrived at the bar at 9:00, about the time I should have been starting on DVD #2, perhaps something set in London and starring Hugh Grant, but nothing so romantic it breaks one down into a fit of tears over one's nonexistent love life. No, something sporty and fun and hip, just right for the Anglophile within us all. Instead, I was forced to endure a frothy pink concoction with fruit in it while listening to each of my friends relay what sorts of backpedaling and storytelling and finagling they had to endure with their husbands and children in order to get the evening off to spend with me. Lovely. Me, the only one who could legitimately get there without asking for permission, did not want to be there at all. So, since I (1) didn't want to be there and (2) had to endure the lengthy stories with a silly grin plastered on my face to show that I actually did care, and (3) was receiving a night filled with drinks for which I did not have to pay, one pink drink turned into two, turned into three.

Let me digress here for a moment to fill you in on something: I've never been much of a party drinker. Even in my college days, heavy drinking was not something I chose to do, so I often just held a bottle of beer and occasionally sipped at it, simply to keep people from saying to me, "Dude," (Note: I am not a "Dude." See the shoes. And the earrings. They're floral.) "where's your drink?" With a warm bottle of beer before me, I was left in peace to watch the strangeness that is a college party. This was my part in college party life.

These days, I do occasionally have some wine with my DVDs, and I've come to appreciate a good vintage with the proper cheese, but not in the froufrou stuffy way. I will not go on about the bouquet or the lingering notes of berry or the smoky overtones. I will, however, be heard to say things such as, "Wow, this is really good. Was it less than ten dollars?" That's as far as that goes. In summary, wine = yes; multicolored mixed concoctions = no.

Which brings us back to the bar with my friends, me three sheets to the wind. Keep in mind my friends have never seen me like this before. They were surprised to learn that their dearly beloved friend knows all, yes, all, the words to Carole King's album Tapestry, and that she can stop and start at about any point therein. Surprisingly, this bar did not have that horrid karaoke thing in the corner, but it turns out they're willing to work with you if you can do A

Natural Woman at top volume with your shoes off. Apparently, I'm pretty good at that one.

Another big surprise (and here I'll tell you that I'm just as surprised as the next person) is that I'm really good at stand up comedy. I guess if I really get going, I have a whole host of dirty jokes and can do an extensive and hilarious (or so I'm told) routine which involves a long list of filthy words, along with their true meanings. This routine involves a fast paced monologue and lots of hand gestures, and it was so wildly popular with the bar's clientele that I've been offered a regular gig in their popular Friday night slot. I've also learned that if you entertain the entire clientele of a bar, thus keeping them there and paying for more drinks, your drinks are suddenly more forthcoming. The friends no longer have to keep a tab running; the bar is more than happy to provide this service for you.

Did you know there's a drink called the Rum Runner? I did not. It's surprisingly refreshing.

We closed the bar, which I've never done before, and I am told I had a lot of fun shouting to the entire crowd to "get the hell out." It was all in good humor, and I guess I signed a few autographs before the place cleared out.

The rest of the night is a bit hazy to me. No, let me rephrase that: The rest of the night is lost to me. My endearing friends took pictures at every turn, then they got them all printed out and made me a lovely coffee table book which I keep under lock and key. They were more than happy, though, to present it to me along with all the stories of what I missed. Such as this one: Upon entering the cab to go home, I removed my panties (grandma panties — I hadn't planned on any sort of show, but there you have it) and placed them on the cab driver's head as some sort of hat. I then mooned several passing cars, puked out the taxi window at a red light, weeped uncontrollably while mourning the breakup with my first serious boyfriend (this occurred 10 years ago), and threatened to get a Mohawk and move to Piccadilly Square. Fortunately, my friends didn't have enough cab fare to get me to the airport, or I'm afraid I may have done so, by the looks of me in the pictures. I had no idea I could do that to my face with lipstick.

At some point, my friends all had to get back home to their husbands and children; the husbands were surprisingly understanding, having received text updates with accompanying photos throughout the evening. For this I am eternally humiliated. But first they got me home and in bed, then stole my car keys and locked me in the apartment with strict instructions to the night doorman not to let me out. That might explain why I instead chose to decorate the inside of my apartment with the remainder of a bottle of cheese-in-a-can and some Fruit Loops.

To say that I had a hangover the next morning is so gross an exaggeration that even typing the words makes me want to vomit a bit. The first thing I noticed upon awakening was a complete and total loss of sensation in my legs. It seems all the feeling lost from there had migrated to the general area of my brain, which thumped and pulsated like a spastic colon. Light blinded me and I could not move my arms for fear of heaving my stomach violently from my body. I do believe I laid in the same position for at least twenty minutes, making a sort of humming noise somewhere deep in my throat, before I had to bolt for the bathroom.

I will spare you the details and allow you to fill in the blanks. Just make sure the blanks include much pain, agony, and retching sounds loud enough to be heard by both the apartment above and the apartment below, thus triggering a flurry of calls to the concierge that the woman in 4C was strangling cats in her bathtub.

It took many days for me to begin to feel myself again. I even called in sick to work for two days. I drank herbal teas, ate nothing but toast, and ended up watching three days of DVDs, including most of Hugh Grant's films. I doubt that I will ever again have a birthday celebration like that again. I also vow to lay low during all the major holidays, and that I shall celebrate with nothing stronger than soda water. The only good thing that has arisen from this entire fiasco is my new job moonlighting. I kill at stand-up.

The Obvious Choice

The sign out front said "Harvey Cragle, Hypnotist." The sign inside said, "Please take a seat. We'll be with you in a moment." Harvey couldn't afford a receptionist yet, but he was working on it. Business was picking up. One may conjecture it was the ad he placed on the side of city bus #127, his large and smiling face above the left rear mud flap promising "Health and Healing to Your Weary Mind." And perhaps that did have something to do with the uptick in clients. But it didn't have everything to do with it.

One Monday morning, several months previous, Harvey's first client was a housewife from Poughkeepsie who told him on the phone that her life felt meaningless. She wanted him to supply her with a sense of meaning, a life worth living outside of carpools and remembering to empty the lint trap so the house didn't burn down.

It was a tall order, but Harvey was sure he could provide.

The first appointment was generally a 15-minute consultation, wherein Harvey discovered exactly what the client hoped to get out of the session. This was followed by a 30-minute hypnosis and then 15 minutes in which Harvey did nothing but let the client sleep while he paid his bills, made phone calls, and played Angry Birds.

Today was no different. Mrs. Farnsworth came into the office where his special comfy chair awaited her, a lush purple velour that gave the impression of a dreamlike space. That, combined with a small crystal mobile in a sunny window, was enough to give most people the feeling he actually knew what he was doing. "Trust," he told himself. "Purple instills trust."

Once Mrs. Farnsworth (she insisted on Lydia) was seated, Harvey got to work and sank her back into alpha state, with the help of a meditation CD that provided the sounds of a Buddhist temple that he'd made himself by sneaking some binaural microphones into a Zen garden a few blocks away. He found that the recording of a trickling waterfall and some chimes were quite lovely, despite the occasional sound of an airplane flying over or a zealous child taunting the koi.

After the usual 30 minutes of past life regression mumbo jumbo, Harvey left Lydia to snooze while he called downtown for Thai food. He was in the mood for something spicy and coconutty, and being quite hungry, he placed a double order to be delivered within the hour. Lunch plans being settled, he pulled Lydia from the depths of beta and sent her on her way, her wallet $50 lighter. As she passed out the door, she commented that all this hypnosis had made her unusually hungry. She was thinking pad thai. Or perhaps a nice coconut curry, thank you very much, goodbye.

These words left Harvey frozen in place on the nappy green carpet. He'd often made phone calls during sessions, but usually it was a round of arguments with his local Internet provider, which meant he spent the bulk of the time on hold waiting for someone to care that he was dissatisfied with his service. Occasionally, he'd just check his voice mail. But most of the time he stuck with Angry Birds. That may have explained one client's need to squeal like a pig before exiting his office, and while that event did cause a chill to run down Harvey's spine, he pretty much just wrote it off as blocked nasal passages.

Now, however, with Lydia Farnsworth heading out to calm a craving for coconut, he had other thoughts. And with all thoughts of this nature, Harvey decided it was best to explore them further. It was fortunate for him that the next appointment was already seated in the waiting room, perusing a battered copy of Past Life Regression Today. He motioned Boris

Leventhal to the back.

Boris was a good natured fellow and one of Harvey's few regulars. Boris felt that a weekly hypnosis session aided him in facing his fears of skittering insects and toothpaste, two things that struck terror into his heart since childhood. This was visually apparent, not so much with the insect thing, but his teeth were deplorable. Harvey had compassion but kept his distance.

Once Boris was settled in and comfortably floating somewhere above his consciousness, Harvey began singing the praises for GlimmerTime Tooth Polish, a new product on the market targeted to people with sensitive gums. He chose this brand because of the catchy tune on the commercial; that, and the spokeswoman was smoking hot. He liked thinking about her while he sang the ditty, "GlimmerTime is all I need to stop my gums whenever they bleed." He sang the song about three times through, then gave Boris the rest of the 27-minute session to snooze while

Harvey picked out a new flatware pattern from an Oneida catalog.

When Boris awoke from his twilight state, he smiled then licked his teeth. Turning from Harvey, he cupped his hand over his mouth and huffed, then paid his bill and left. Harvey couldn't help but smile when he heard the faint humming of the GlimmerTime jingle as Boris bounced out of the office. He had no doubt his client's next stop was Paul's Pharmacy two doors down.

Harvey had no other appointments that day, but he did have several more scattered throughout the week, thanks to a coupon in the Sunday flier (first hypnosis 50% off, plus a free Franz Anton Mesmer poster). He was looking forward to testing his blooming idea.

As the week wore on, he convinced Mr. Plotnik that the cause for his anxiety at work was due to a lack of a pair of Florsheim shoes, which would offer fine arch support. Ms. Del Rey left his office and went straight to her local FTD florist to order expensive bouquets for everyone she'd wronged in her years as a hobbyist shoplifter. And little 12-year-old Tommy Grunswick practically bounced out the door, the newfound cure to his ADHD having been discovered: In a past life, he was the inventor of the Lego and thus had a sudden urge to fill his room with various kits and such, his relieved mother all too happy to oblige.

With this powerful evidence before him, Harvey knew he had only one thing left to do: sell ad spots. He produced spreadsheets, gathered data, and created PowerPoint presentations until he was ready to meet with some real heavy hitters. AT&T was the first one out of the box, giving him a budget of $100,000 with which to suggest clients needed better cell phone coverage in order to assuage their mental anguish. Next up was Prudential, coming in with a $200,000 budget. People needed the security that only good insurance could provide. The real surprise was McDonald's. He knew they'd have the advertising dollars to toss his way, but a shocking $750,000, just to hum the theme song and whisper, "I'm lovin' it" would be enough to finance his dream home.

Perhaps he should have felt a prick in his conscience. Maybe he should have lost a bit of sleep at night. But Harvey didn't. He slept like a babe on his fine new percale sheets, and his conscience was clear. As he began the advertising campaign with his clients, he saw a large increase in success. Most people wanted to be told what to like, what to buy. Most people longed for the excitement nothing but a new game console could bring. And since the pleasure of a new shiny thing was only temporary, this meant lots of repeat business for Harvey Cragle, Hypnotist. While it's true none of his clients knew what was up, the rush of a purchase to come was a powerful thing. No one seemed to make the tie-in. And the investors were only too happy to continue throwing dough his way, Harvey only too happy to catch it.

Things would have continued in this manner, blissfully profitable, if it weren't for the sale at Macy's. He had a funny feeling he should never advertise a sale, but it was a quick and tidy sum that he only needed to implant mentally for a week at most. Black Friday sale, they said. One week only, they said. Starts a week before Thanksgiving, so he thought they said.

Perhaps if Harvey had been a more astute consumer himself, he would have understood just what Black Friday was. It sounded so funereal, he never would have imagined it was the beginning of a shopper's paradise weekend. And, perhaps, if Harvey hadn't spent every day after Thanksgiving lounging on the couch reading hypnotist journals and soothing holiday indigestion, he would have been more acutely aware of the chaos and pandemonium that is Black Friday. Perhaps this would have riveted into his brain the day on which it actually fell.

Instead, somewhere between filling out masses of paperwork and depositing large sums into offshore accounts, he lost track of the days, hence dumping his Macy's schedule on its head. Since the holidays are an especially busy time for a hypnotist, or anyone in the mental field, for that matter, Harvey's time slots were booked full up. Clients were scheduled back to back, and his waiting room was packed at all times. He even hired a temp secretary to get him through until he could procure more permanent help. The temp was at wit's ends most days, just trying to keep apart the kleptomaniacs and those with delusions of grandeur. One afternoon, it took her 45 minutes to untangle a depressed yoga instructor from an angry young philanthropist who were fighting over a copy of Reader's Digest.

Somewhere in the office melee, Harvey picked up the paperwork for the Macy's sale from his desk and started feeding it to his hypnotized clients. "Big sale starting Friday. Macy's. Bargain buster, won't last long, sparkling holiday goodness," etc. There was something about the gleam in their eyes as each left his office that let him know they'd not only taken the bait, but would head right home to mark the date on their calendars.

What awaited the Macy's staff that following Friday morning at 6 a.m. looked more like a tired campout of Woodstock revelers. This was a true sign of the uptick in clients Harvey had experienced, and their enthusiasm over his ability to fix what ailed them was written all over their eager faces. In fact, the enthusiasm over the sale was so intense in each of his post hypnotic people that their lust for rock bottom prices had rubbed off on just about anyone of any significance in their lives. Throughout the preceding night, they'd shown up in droves, bringing along wives and husbands, sleepy children, neighbors, mothers and fathers. Bundled up from head to toe in appropriate cold weather wear, the excited crowd hardly slept in their tents at all, but instead swapped stories about what might be awaiting them within the store's walls.

Lo and behold, the store did not open at 6 a.m. as the crowd somehow sensed it would. The bundled would-be shoppers shuffled their tired anticipatory feet. They began to mumble. "What is this malarkey?" they cried in consternation. "Where is this sale of which we suspect?" and from the back, "I want leg warmers!"

Shaking the doors did not help, unless you consider tripping the alarm system being of any assistance. Which the police department most certainly did. It wasn't long before a cop car pulled slowly into the parking lot, took one look at the mass of humanity shaking their wallets, then put the car into reverse to hide on the other side of the store while calling for backup.

Officer Drumble requested the SWAT team but was denied it with a laugh. No, two more cars would be sent. Until those two cars arrived and requested the SWAT team and the fire department and possibly a helicopter.

A helicopter was indeed sent, but it was not the nice police unit with the cool flashing lights and the computerized bullhorn. It was the news chopper from T.V. 8, and boy, was the newscaster excited. This excitement, which had built from the crowd below and had filtered up through the air and, despite the chop, chop, chop of the blades, made its way into Bill's already excited newscaster cranium. Shouting the news into his microphone, he gave coverage of what appeared to be a massive Black Friday-type crowd, which was suspect considering it was mid November.

Harvey, sitting on his couch enjoying his morning coffee, had flipped the television on in a rare attempt to catch the weather report. Instead, he got an onslaught of hyped up coverage on the pending nonsale at Macy's. This is where Harvey dropped his coffee on his brand new Karistan rug. This is where Harvey ran to his new iPhone and checked his calendar. This is where Harvey realized his catastrophic mistake.

Pulling on an LL Bean sweater, a North Face parka, and an Eddie Bauer hat, he ran from the house and hopped into his new Mercedes Benz SL. He raced straight to Macy's but had quite a time of getting close enough to the crowd to see. By this time, the store manager and 12 dazed employees clustered around a police car wondering what to do. The police assured them the doors must stay closed, but the store manager saw nothing but the possibility of a pre-pre holiday push, possibly an award or plaque of some kind at the yearly Christmas party.

Harvey's Pioneer stereo system piped out the breaking news and informed him that there was talk of a Black Friday sale, poorly timed on the part of Macy's. His teeth began to rattle and his iPhone began to jingle. Macy's advertising department. No big surprise there. He was going to toss the phone right out the window but decided to face the music.

"Yes? Yes, this is he.... I do apologize, sir, I...yes, I see...you want me to what?" He got out of the car still clinging his phone and crossed the parking lot with tentative steps. Stopping at the police car, he awaited the officer's notice. Then he handed the officer the phone, who said "Yes, uh-huh, I understand" a few times before handing it to the store manager. This was repeated but with more glee on the manager's part until the call was ended. Then the manager reached into his pocket, raised his large keyring before his employees, and jangled them like Santa heading skyward. The employees shrank back in fear, but the manager showed aplomb. Borrowing a megaphone from the officer, he forced his way to the front of the store, and the crowd magically parted, a Red Sea of patrons awaiting Clearance prices. But before the manager unlocked the doors, he turned to the crowds and shouted through the megaphone.

"Today is an extra special event — 25% off

everything in store, even clearance items!" The crowd hooted and hollered. They pushed forward, but the man with the keys gestured them back and they obeyed.

What followed looked somewhat like a funnel effect, the parking lot emptying of people and the store accepting them, doors open wide like a hungry mouth. The scene elicited plenty of jittery rhetoric from the news chopper, who relayed in ecstasy the store's decision to open its doors early this morning. People in their homes, still half dressed and sipping coffee, began making calls to their offices and factories to say that ...ahem... they felt a little under the weather and would not be able to come to work today. Macy's had its biggest pre-pre holiday sale-sale in its history. The store manager got his plaque. And Harvey?

Harvey's business boomed. His ad clients ranged from Coca-Cola to the Prince of Brunei hoping for some extra PR. And people from all over the tristate area drove in to be hypnotized by him, excited by the prospect of feeling excited. No one could explain the phenomenon, but all knew that they had quite the rush after seeing him; and that they needed to return weekly or they'd lose it.

Harvey ended up with a very large office in the highest building of the city. Top floor. He bought expensive Steelcase office furniture, leather of course, and hired not one but three full time receptionists, a filing clerk, and an ad writer who posed as a janitor, just to keep things on the down low.

Oftentimes, Harvey would sit home in the evenings and reflect on the bizarre turn of events. What had happened? What was to be learned from this, if anything? He felt it bubbling under the surface, but it never erupted into his brain. Perhaps he held it back. Perhaps. But for now, he'd just sit back on his VIG Chesterfield leather sofa, enjoy his new Sony 84" television with Grand Enigma surround sound, and sip at a Baccarat crystal glass of Glenfarclas.

Real Names from Real Phone Books

I used to work as a proofreader for a phone book company. Whenever I would tell someone that I read phone books for a living, that I spent countless hours poring over the white pages, it always garnered the same reaction. There would be a look of disbelief followed by shock, followed by what I translated to be pity. Because it is just as boring as it sounds. Someone must read each and every name in the phone book; someone must make sure there are no typos in the words "street" or "avenue" or "Cincinnati." Someone needs to make sure every phone number has seven digits; that there is a little dash between the first three and the last four of said digits; that each person's name is in bold type and the rest that follows is not.

Now, my particular office produced phone books for cities all over the country. At our company's height, we had a staff of eight proofreaders, all sitting in little cubicles with large galleys on their desks and red pens in their hands. Most of us would have rather been home writing a novel or screenplay; we were thus a squirrelly bunch. So when we came across a funny name, it was a highly entertaining occasion and we had to shared it with one another. I began cataloging the names as a way to pass the time. My coworkers were only too happy to help me with my unusual collection. At one point, we started wondering if it weren't all some big cosmic joke. Perhaps these people weren't real after all. Maybe these were stage names. Or maybe someone at the national residential listings database was playing a big prank on us. So when we first bumped up against the name Astroflash Jones, one of my coworkers decided to give this person a call.

It was a woman. And she was not pleased that we had questioned her validity. In fact, she was so highly offended that we opted not to verify unusual names anymore. (These were the days before Google and Facebook.)

And, lest I further upset Ms. Astroflash, let me reassure you: No matter how unusual any of these names may appear, in most cases, there is more than one person out there with that very name. Countless are the Jack Frosts and the Cary Grants and the Sweetie Pies. Betty Boop? There are several. Mona Bolona? Surprisingly, there's more than one. Koots Dronkers? I'm not sure. But I will tell you this: If you find the name of your uncle or your cousin or your neighbor or even yourself, I apologize right now. Bud Light, I'm sorry I'm making fun of your name. Emma Bemmajemma Shubin and LaCraCha Handy? I'm sorry for finding humor where you find only your monikers. Bland Couch? Stop complaining. Your name is far from mundane.

I'm sure you business owners will take a totally different viewpoint to this list and welcome any attention brought forth. The Curl Up & Dye Hair Salon, for instance; or Dairy Aire Operations. Bacon & Rice CPAs, Elbows & Derriers (what they do, I'm at a loss), Gol-De-Rocks & Momma Bear Jewelers; Petal Pusher (a florist); the consignment shop Danielle's Steals; Camelback Chiropractic; House of Burns Memorial Chapel; Doggie Doo PU Service; Slavic Butcher & Baecker Construction; Grumpy Stumper (stump removal service); Go With the Flow Colon Hydrotherapy; Poopy's Potties; Sukup & Grimm (attorneys); Arnt U Gladufoundus; Fubar Corporation; Delta Hair Lines; and the favorite of everyone down at the office, Master Bait & Tackle; I wish you all the best.

Sometimes the business names are seen to their advantage when accompanied by their slogan. Such is the case with Budget Electric: Let Us Remove Your Shorts. And then there's Vacuum Doctor: We Deal With Dirtbags and Suckers.

Some of the greatest finds were the listings for doctors. Need an OB/GYN? Try Dr. Menapase. Dentist? How about Dr. Smiley? Then there's Dr. Stitcha, Dr. Nurse, Dr. Doctor, Dr. Gutstein (a gastroenterologist), Dr. Rectanus (a psychologist, but perhaps he specializes in anal retentiveness), Dr. Gutts, Dr. Butts (an oral surgeon, so wrong end there), even a Dr. Frankenstein. Then there's Dr. Croak, Dr. Hacker, and Dr. Maludy.

But let's get back to the residential listings, shall we? That's where most of the action was. We could almost put these names into categories. For instance, take the rhyming and/or repetitive names such as Amico Damico, Bill Dill, Thomas Thomas, Crago Crago, Celeste West, Geik Geiken, Vito Zito, Jack Hack. Margarita Capuchina has a nice ring to it. Then there's Cookie Cook, None None, Dottie Doody, Billy Gilley, Vickey Wickey, Cha Cha, and Satin Satin.

Or how about names with double meanings? In this category, you'd find Kinda

Lowe, I.M. Bright, Iva Chance, G. Eye, Chuck Cole, B. Myself, I.M. Polish, Iva Head, Did Her, I.M. Kinder, Holli Roller, B. Sure, Foster A. Boyle, and Paris Frantz.

Fictional characters? That one's easy. Here we have Pebbles Flintstone, Fozzie Bear, Andy Griffith, Bevis Butthead, Daisy Duck, and Captain Marvel.

Famous names abound (and there are usually many listings across the country for each of these): Gary Cooper, Betty Davis, James Dean, Jimmy Stewart, Bennie Goodman, Pink Floyd, and Johann Sebastian Bach, just to name a few. We won't even bother with the likes of Michael Jackson or James Brown. Not a book went by without a solid dozen of each.

Names based on weather patterns, seasons, and nature were quite popular: Willow Dawn, April December, Misty Lake, Tuesday Summers, Autumn Barefoot, Star Bright, April Rainey, Rainee Knight; Smokey Rain; Sandy Beach;

Autumn Weathers, Forest Peet,

And then there were the just plain odd: Shocker Dabish, Bushee Dabney, Nickersear Doyle, Big Doc Fulwiley, Tuesday Galloway, Method Gavura, Budzinski Gebhart, Urban Cumberbatch. There was Kind David, Lonely Eugene Gooseby, Funk McCracken. And Handy Helen, Ecstacy Rivera, Eboni White, Perpetual Williams. And who could forget Zeke ZZZYPT? And Baby Frank. And Shithaus Britter. Dull Dan. Killastain Day. Harmony Labouncy, Lita Lamb, Raymond Zin (who I can only imagine went by Ray Zin), Ajax Vartanian, and Wesley Whimper. Socrates Diamond and MT Smack McDonald.

Occasionally, a residential listing would be followed by a person's occupation. Such was the case with Hasty Brian, auctioneer; Dusty Waterman, plumber; Amy Miracle, midwife.

Putting two unrelated nouns together is always an interesting way to create a good name, so future parents take note: Million Gray,

Reversal Grant, Regional Garland, Crystal Cotton, King Chow, Pinkey Bell, Royal Prince, Violet Haze, Fuchsia Pink, Skip Frosty, Apple Pie, Sandy Candy. Guardian Angel has a listing, which is nice to know. (I like that they can be easily accessed.) Cookie Dress (which kind of sounds like a crummy outfit; sorry for that one, but it couldn't be ignored so I said it for you); Fuzzy Fries, Minnie Franks, Cinnamon Pope. Groovy Train, Fine Time, Dallas Mustard, Destiny Flower, Rusty Bell. Then there's Summer Pet, Melon Price, Blue Fish, Royal Gentz, Rivets Drummer. Rockie Fish, Fine Time, Crummie Birdie, Misty Graves, Fig Dial, Velvet Wonder, Icy Hill, Lady Lovely, Valentine Fish, Royal Stoner, Moody Leach, Jock Felt, Lucky Fly, Violet Love, Salty Slyce. Don't forget Harry Bacon, Lucky Monk, Wade Pooler, and Wednesday Sheets.

And here are a few clever first names; imagine a mother calling these children in for dinner: Ostrich. Future. Crochetta. Dinks. Brix.

Drucilla. Evil (not advised.) Buckmaster. Menthal. Stump. Tangerine. Huggybear. Tootles. Minute. Twinette. Mystery. Paradise.

Married couples are always fun. If you're named Jim and Jam, for instance. Or Louis and Louise. Chip and Dale. Rocky and Robin. Joe and Flo Cool; Speed and Bunny; Jerry and Gerri Chevery; and, of course, Jack and Jill.

Keeping in mind that names are listed last name first within a phone book, sometimes the results of this flip-flop are highly entertaining. Take these, for instance: Grim, Reaper; Lima, BN; Hey, You; Pick, Up; Pickup, Itsme; Good, BM; Green, T; Goodnight, Gracie (reach back in your radio show history for that last one); Nass, Carl; English, Guy; and Uneeda, Bath.

The politically incorrect made appearances in the pages of a phone book, as well. Major Fagg must spend a lot of time explaining his moniker. Eggfou Young probably gets a few nasty looks. Dam Hung must have it pretty hard, too. I'm not sure if it's politically incorrect, but the political agenda certainly hangs tight on Elekta Gore, as does Clinton Crum.

If anyone needs a phone number these days, we're more likely to hop on the net and just Google it. It's much quicker, but there's something lost in not being able to scan down the pages. You can't go look yourself up to see how your name looks in print. You can't make a quick check to see if your ex-girlfriend is still married to that loser and living on 8th Avenue. And you can't make any accidental discoveries. Do I ever get the urge to sit down with a good phone book and read it? I'm going to say no to that. But I do miss being able to add to my collection. For all of you who think I've listed you above, don't sweat it. Instead, receive the heartfelt thanks of me and all my old coworkers. You are probably the only reason we were able to pick up that red pen day after day and face another 800-page phone book.

Life of an Artist

While I do understand this class assignment was to bring to life a well-known artist, I wanted to expound on someone that should have been a well-known artist, but like so many hard working and devoted painters throughout history, this one slipped through the cracks. It is my intention to eradicate this oversight, thus undoing a grievous error of the art world.

During my backpacking travels across Europe last year to get serious and find my manhood, as my father encouraged, I came upon the story of an artist who was a sculptor. Wait, a painter. I heard about him while visiting a remote Italian cathedral — no, French. It was French. This French cathedral, while in serious disrepair, contains several works of art that would appear in art history books if only the ash and decay of time would be carefully removed. Alas, this cathedral is so remote it doesn't have a name, so no sense in trying to find it on Wikipedia. Nor will the artist, Pierre La Fontainbleau, appear in any Wikipedia entries. (I am currently trying to rectify this situation, but so far my attempts have done nothing but get me banned from adding a wiki, that pompous and elitist group of WikiMasters claiming they need more "substantial proof." What a crock.)

The story of Pierre La Fontainbleau was told to me by the grounds keeper of the unnamed cathedral, whose broken English was occasionally translated to me through the help of a lovely French woman I met named Mademoiselle La Boef. My traveling companion, my foreign lover, my muse, Mademoiselle La Boef spent much time in translating the grounds keeper's story, as Pierre La Fontainbleau was his great grandfather on his mother's side.

Pierre was born to a poor sheepherder who was unable to provide his young artistic son with a paint set, so young Pierre began dabbling in sheep dip. By the age of twelve, his renderings were viewed by the townspeople as something of a local wonder. As paper could not be afforded either, the artwork was done on nearby rocks and cobblestone walkways, which as you can imagine, was washed away by the rain. Even today, you can find old timers sipping wine and eating fetid cheese who can tell you about Pierre's early works, lost to the inclement weather of the region before his mother consented to allowing him to paint within the house, decorating walls, floor, and ceiling in lively images of dancing girls, skipping oxen, and fanciful fields of flowers.

By the age of 16, Pierre was quite adept at mixing the sheep dip to allow for maximum variation of browns and tans. Eventually, the village rector, who would no longer visit the family abode claiming the stench within burned the hairs of his nostrils, purchased a set of paints, an easel, and the stretched canvases that became

La Fontainbleau's first full color works. Oddly, the subject matter pivoted from the aforementioned lasses and oxen to piles of colorful sheep dip, perhaps La Fontainbleau's attempt to reach back into his childhood artistic beginnings. While these works did indeed smell a heap better than those previous, the subject matter was not as much of a draw to the local farmers and craftsmen who did not understand avante garde (which is ironic, if you think about it, seeing as this phrase originates from the French for "avante garde.")

By the time La Fontainbleau was 21, the nearby cathedral was finished and was in dire need of interior beautification. Under strict supervision from the priest who, under no circumstances wanted a sheep dip motif within, Pierre set about painting the walls and ceiling with an effluvium of patterns and colors unlike that which had ever been seen before. Casting aside what was up until that time the "de rigeur" for churches, cathedrals, and other buildings used for Christian worship that I can't think of the names for right now, Pierre's designs were new and fresh, albeit slightly disturbing to the community who were really expecting and looking forward to the standard issue angels, trumpets, heaven and hell sort of thing European cathedrals were known for. So there was a bit of a problem there, and before Pierre was able to complete his project, he was summarily booted out onto the street with nothing more than his tattered old paintbrushes and his trusty yet well worn beret. (Rumor has it it was an odd raspberry color, which later inspired the artist formerly known as Prince. But one can only conjecture. I attempted to contact said artist; alas he has refused to reply to my emails. I did sign up for his newsletter, though, and it's interesting when it does show up, which is rarely. Big disappointment here. Whatever happened to Prince? Where is he now? Do doves cry?)

As you can well imagine, Pierre was

besotted, beside himself, and having fits of general malaise. He traveled to Paris where he found a tiny hovel around the corner from an absinthe bar. The grounds keeper, who you will remember is the great grandson of La Fontainbleau, told me that there was even one instance where he came face to face with the great Vincent Van Gogh, immediately forging a strong and lasting friendship. According to family legend, Pierre tried intensely to discourage Van Gogh from the removal of his ear, but the distraught artist would have none of that. He said if he was to make a mark on the world, it may not be through his art but in the painful removal of a part of himself. (The grounds keeper tried to convince me that La Fontainbleau himself kept the ear bits in a small box under the floorboards but accidentally forgot them when he moved from Paris in the spring of 1889. At one point, I thought I'd tracked down the Parisian hovel, but the landlady would not allow me to pull up the floorboards stating something to the effect of "La merde, blah blah oui non non," but my translator Mademoiselle La Boef was not present at the time, having left me in the countryside for the grounds keeper's handsome son named Louis or Francois or some other very pretentious and annoying name.)

After Pierre left Paris distraught and without Van Gogh's ear, he wandered back toward the countryside only to discover that, after nearly 10 year's absence, not only was the town pretty much done for (there had been a nasty tapeworm epidemic that left most of the townspeople bereft of feeling, hence the shaving of heads commenced. Humiliated, their innate sense of French fashion causing them to seek solace within the neighboring convents and monasteries where baldness was not only accepted but revered for its holiness) but even the La Fontainbleau family had deserted the area, leaving no forwarding address, until our fearless grounds keeper's father returned years later to search for his roots and a possible fortune in ancient sheep herding tools for which his family was known. Alas, no tools were uncovered.

It is part of La Fontainbleau family lore that Pierre left a few of his works with Vincent Van Gogh as payment for several rounds of absinthe and a few Parisian women of the evening, and that Van Gogh, being severely confused at this point from having been Van Gogh since birth, signed his own name to them and passed them off as his own work. Something to do with sunflowers and night and stars, but I cannot entirely recall, having been under the influence of the grounds keeper's very strong brandy which I'm pretty sure would be illegal here in the states. At least, that's the impression I got from the hangover the next day.

La Fontainbleau's story ends tragically, as all good French artists' do. Finding himself penniless and without a home, only the tattered remnants of a beret to cover his thinning hair, Pierre half walked and half crawled to his old family home, now empty but for a few smeared sheep dip doodles still clinging to the dusty walls. There he stayed until his passing at the age of 42. Legend has it he was found dead near the hearth, clutching a frazzled paintbrush and a bucket of sheep dip. The cause of death was unknown, although some claim there was a bit of hemlock cud tucked between his cheek and jaw.

As I said at the beginning of this report, the cathedral still stands. Well, most of it, anyway. I could never figure out why such a dilapidated building required a grounds keeper, and being a foreigner, I was too embarrassed to ask. But from what I could tell by peering into the unlit and dank interior, the swirls and dots of color, although faded, were a bit of a disappointment. Quite frankly, I, too, was hoping for angels and trumpets. Maybe a few men in pointy hats trimmed in gold leaf.

Still, you'll notice I now sport a raspberry beret to class each and every day, my little reminder to myself that sometimes life is magical and artistic, and at other times it's just full of shit.

The Art of Gumshoe

It was almost time to close up shop. I knew because I could hear the booze calling me. Perhaps something light and refreshing. Like a mojito. Just as I was about to flip the sign to Closed, the bell over the door tinkled and in walked a gorgeous redhead. Or maybe she was blond, it was hard to tell through the waves of sex appeal bouncing off my corneas.

"You Sid?" she asked, hip-swiveling herself over to my desk.

"There are lots of guys named Sid, baby," I wisecracked. "Name's Club. Sid Club."

She sat down and crossed her legs. I heard a siren go off in the back of my brain.

"Have a seat, why don't you." I took a long look at her longer legs and then finished flipping the sign to Closed.

"Mr. Club," she said, striking a match on my No Smoking sign and lighting a cigarette as long as the Nile, "I've got a problem."

"Don't we all." I sat on the edge of my desk and unwrapped a caramel. Seemed I had a problem, too, and I was looking at her.

"I need your help. Something of mine has gone missing, and I want you to find it." She looked at me all doe eyed, in that way dames like her always do, so I did what any red blooded male in my situation would do: I chewed harder on my caramel.

"What's missing, honey?"

"I've lost my sense of purpose. I've looked for it everywhere, and I've come to one unnerving conclusion: I think someone swiped it."

"When's the last time you saw it? You know, they always say you should retrace your steps. Maybe it rolled under the couch. Or perhaps you left it on the subway. That happens sometimes."

"Mr. Club, don't take me for a fool. I checked under the couch twice and I don't take the subway. I even had the dog x-rayed."

"In that case, you've come to the right place," I said, doing a mental jig on what I'd bill her. I threw in some extra for mojito money and maybe some argyle socks. "Where should I start? Any ideas?"

"I have a nasty feeling my ex-boyfriend might have something to do with this. You'll want to talk with him. His name is Patsy Falafel." She grabbed my pen and wrote his address on the palm of her hand. I wondered if this meant she was coming with me. "He's a former ping pong champion with a swing like a Japanese tourist, so watch your step. And if you get a chance to get in his apartment, do me a favor and look for my dignity. I think I left it there with my grandma's earrings."

"Sounds like a real gem. The boyfriend, I mean. What's his angle?"

"He never wanted me to do anything meaningful in life. He kept trying to convince me to join the ping pong racket with him, polish balls, that sort of thing."

"Doesn't sound very rewarding."

"Exactly," she said. She stubbed her cigarette out in my handmade ashtray, the one I carefully crafted back in first grade. It hadn't been used since my mother died while rubbing a cigarette out in it. I flinched.

"Sorry," she said, "I thought it was an ashtray."

"Don't worry," I said, not bothering to explain, "I'll have it reupholstered."

She reached over and started wiping the ashtray out with the hem of her dress. Then she moved on to sorting my mail as she filled me in on all the sordid details: How her high school teacher was the first to give her a sense of purpose, how she'd taken it to college with her, clung to it in her first years on her own trying to make it as a torch singer in a seedy nursery school. Finally, she'd met Falafel and fallen head over high heels. Then, the purpose simply vanished without a trace.

By the time she finished her sad story, she had half my office organized. As she put the finishing touches on alphabetizing my paper clips, I knew I'd take the case. How could I not, after she went to all the trouble of shining my Rolodex?

"How about we make a little trade off? I'll take the case and you stick around, maybe do some secretarial work?"

"I'm a modern woman, Mr. Club. I don't do secretarial work."

"Office manager, then."

Her eyes lit up like Christmas at Macy's as she gave my office the once-over. She walked around a few minutes, flipping through files, organizing receipts, and finally stopping at a map of the city, all the bars and jazz joints circled in red Sharpie. A smile spread across her face for a moment, and I thought for certain she would accept. As certain as a pig tap dancing on ice cream bars. At the last moment, she whirled around to face me, a Walther P22 gripped in her perfectly manicured hand.

"Where'd you get it, you scumbag?"

I was taken aback, but not so far I lost control. I wasn't ready to bite the linoleum just yet — I still had a mojito coming to me. "Get what, Ms. Wanderlust?"

"My sense of purpose! How did you know I'd come here looking for it?"

"I'm not sure I know what you mean," I said, "I didn't take your sense of purpose. Maybe you never really lost it to begin with. Maybe it was stuck to the bottom of your shoe, like a bit of toilet tissue. Or gum."

"I don't believe that for a minute. You know what I think, Mr. Club? I think this is a setup." She waved the gun around, pointing at my desk, the city map, even the box of Lincoln Logs I kept in the corner for the slow times. "You think you can have me that easy, eh?"

"Now, listen here," I said, backing away

slowly, hoping to get close enough to my staple gun to really let her have it, "You shoot me, and your sense of purpose goes with me, see? What'll you do then, hang around my empty office? Rewind the typewriter ribbons? Who'll mess the paper clips back up again?"

"I'll get another job. I'll find another sap with another screwed up office, and I'll be tops, got it? I can see it now," she said, getting as glazed over as a jelly doughnut, "I'll computerize everything, start a murder database organized by size of head injury. I'll order business cards with little Sherlock Holmes logos on them. I'll do PR!" She was in a flow. "I can see it now: Newspaper ads, your face on the side of a bus, maybe an evening gala with a live band and hors d'oeuvre shaped like magnifying glasses." I was following along, getting pretty excited myself. I wondered if she'd consider mariachi. I liked mariachi. It went well with mojitos. I had to save this dame, and fast. My books were in the red.

I leaned in hard now, giving it all I had. "If you rub me out, sweetheart, no PI worth his fedora will hire the murderess of hopes and dreams. Think about the implications. The liability insurance."

She thought about it, her gun wavering and her eyebrows twitching. I could feel her about to cave, and once again her eyes started to roam the room. I slowly reached down and picked up a box of #2 pencils I had sitting there — a fresh box, unsharpened. Gingerly, I held them out to her and shook them just enough to make them plink like tiny marimbas. She could see the gleam of the school bus yellow paint. A whiff of graphite reached her dainty nostrils and she sniffed. When her eyes landed on the electric pencil sharpener before me, she set the gun down and picked it up, cradling it to her, stroking the extension cord and cooing.

"Alright then," she said, "but I get my own parking spot."

The Author Bio Outtake Page

Every book includes an author bio, and every author bio reads as if it were written by someone other than the author; the editor, perhaps. Or maybe a publishing house peon, cranking out bios all day long, hoping for a big promotion to back cover text one day. But, no. The burden generally falls on the author who must write something glowing or revealing or slightly braggy about herself. Such was my case.

You might think this is an easy enough task. "Joe Frample is a writer from Louisville, Kentucky, who studied journalism in his basement for 12 years before winning his first Pulitzer. Frample has a wife named Enid and a pet cow named Flaxen. He is 52 years old." But when you're writing about yourself, something funny happens (unless you're a memoirist; then you're used to writing about yourself.) The burden becomes close to overwhelming. "What can I possibly say about myself that anyone would want to hear? Is that too much information? Not enough?" Such are the narcissistic musings of the typical writer.

After much pacing and head scratching (the cover artist was waiting for these simple lines of text, and I'd made her wait long enough), my husband told me to stop worrying, sit down, and crank out several of them in rapid succession. The trick worked; my fingers were loose on the keyboard, just how I like it, and the nonsense wouldn't stop flowing. What resulted was a fine mess, and why I've chosen to leave this with you as your last impression of me is beyond my understanding.

1.) Michelle Sandoval is a writer from Michigan who has mentally traveled to all corners of the universe, including Middle Earth and Xanadu. She likes the upper left corner of her frontal lobe best.

2.) Michelle Sandoval is a writer of humor. She has a husband and a son and a dog and enjoys reading words on any surface.

3.) Michelle Sandoval is a writer who hales from Michigan. She enjoys walks in the woods, music, and sculpting things with cheese.

4.) Michelle Sandoval is a humor writer from Michigan. She has a wonderful husband, an adorable son, and a very long dog.

5.) Michelle Sandoval writes a lot of things. She reads in her spare time, and even when she has no spare time, such as when she is in line at the DMV or while she cooks. She burns a lot of food.

6.) Michelle Sandoval is a humor writer from Michigan who lives with her husband, her young son, a barking dachshund, and three squawking birds. She wears earplugs while she writes.

7.) Michelle Sandoval writes. When she's

not writing, she's reading. If she had not grown up to be a writer, she would have been an astronaut, probably; either that or a ballerina.

8.) Michelle Sandoval is a writer from Michigan who enjoys steamed carrots.

9.) Michelle Sandoval is a humor writer, both online and in print. She aspires to write many more books and to someday put an end to fruit flies. And earwigs.

10.) Michelle Sandoval writes books and pithy tweets and humorous blog posts; sometimes she writes shopping lists and sticky notes to her husband. Otherwise, she's probably off reading something.

11.) Michelle Sandoval is a writer who is tired of trying to come up with an idea for an author bio. She thinks it's enough that she's let everyone into her brain already, to read all that funny stuff that goes on up there. Any more info on her and her readers might lock her up. Or put her in a cage and feed her nothing but bananas.

12.) Michelle Sandoval writes, reads, laughs, folds, types, yells, runs, swats, hugs, and weeps bitterly when someone eats the last of the pretzels.

13.) Michelle Sandoval is a writer. She lives in Michigan and is married to a really neat guy. Her son is neat, too, and said he would like to be mentioned in this bio. She also has a dachshund, who does not care if she's mentioned in the bio or not.

14.) Michelle Sandoval is an author. She lives.

Made in the USA
San Bernardino, CA
30 April 2018